A PLACE FOR US

A PLACE FOR US

Dee Wyatt

Chivers Press • G.K. Hall & Co.
Bath, England   Waterville, Maine USA

This Large Print edition is published by Chivers Press, England, and by G.K. Hall & Co., USA.

Published in 2002 in the U.K. by arrangement with the author.

Published in 2002 in the U.S. by arrangement with Dee Wyatt.

U.K. Hardcover   ISBN 0–7540–4742–3 (Chivers Large Print)
U.K. Softcover   ISBN 0–7540–4743–1 (Camden Large Print)
U.S. Softcover   ISBN 0–7838–9662–X (Nightingale Series Edition)

The text of this Large Print edition is unabridged.
Other aspects of the book may vary from the original edition.

Set in 16 pt. New Times Roman.

Printed in Great Britain on acid-free paper.

British Library Cataloguing in Publication Data available

Library of Congress Cataloging-in-Publication Data

Wyatt, Dee.
    A place for us / by Dee Wyatt.
       p. cm. — (G.K. Hall large print nightingale series)
    ISBN 0–7838–9662–X (lg. print : sc : alk. paper)
    1. Large type books. I. Title. II. Series.
PR6073.Y32 P56 2002
823'.914—dc21   2001039978

CHAPTER ONE

'Well, Aunt Lorna, I'm here! Let's hope your famous crystal ball wasn't having an off-day when it told you to leave this place to me!'

With a wry little frown Carrie Davies stepped out of her car, aware of the fact that she was talking to herself again. She had been doing that a lot lately since Aunt Lorna died, and even more so, it seemed, since Declan had decided he wasn't prepared to offer even a token commitment! And when, three months ago, he finally left her for someone else, Carrie had felt ridiculously upset about it.

She had had her work and, through it, her colleagues, which had helped a little, but she hadn't been able to shake off the misery of rejection, or loneliness. That had been the worst, and Carrie shuddered, still feeling the emptiness.

She no longer missed Declan, but she still felt the loss of Aunt Lorna, even though it had been over a year now since her funeral. She had to admit that, lately, it was gradually beginning to fade and in its place a different feeling was starting to creep in, a feeling of restlessness. Then, one morning the letter arrived . . .

The letter had been sent to her by Aunt Lorna's solicitors, Turpin and Turpin, and it

1

had instructed her to contact them regarding her aunt's estate in the heart of Wales. When she telephoned them she had discovered that she, Miss Caroline Davies, was now the owner of Dell Cottage, along with quite a surprising legacy.

In that moment she knew her new life was about to begin. And arriving here today was the start of it!

Carrie sighed, turning her full attention to the cottage. She closed her eyes momentarily and breathed in the soft, pleasant air. It was still hard for her to believe that she was now the owner of this lovely place, and a place so aptly named, too. The cottage lay in a clearing, isolated beyond the village and surrounded by its own large garden where, beyond the ivied walls, flocks of sheep grazed drowsily. The building was old, low and red-bricked, with yellow roses rambling over the porch, and dog-daisies, which had once seemed to be taller than herself, swaying and dancing in a white and gold profusion. Clouds of lilac completed the picture and everywhere the air hung heavy with the sweet scent of grass.

'Heaven!' Carrie breathed, her excitement now so strong she could almost taste it.

She reached back into the car to lift out two plastic bags, and decided to leave her suitcases until later. She then took the key out of her bag and, delighted as she was, she pondered for the hundredth time what she would actually do with her life now that she was about to live here. Stepping carefully along the paving stones that made up the path, she moved towards the house.

Her eyes were soon drawn towards the conservatory. Yes, it was still there, and still looking very much as she remembered it. This had been one of her favourite places and Carrie found herself moving towards it. It ran directly through the middle of the cottage, separating it from what had long ago been the stables, and which Aunt Lorna had turned into a guest annexe, although as far as Carrie could remember, no guests had ever been invited.

Squinting through the windows, she could see that the long table where she and Aunt Lorna ate their breakfasts was still there, and still covered by its vinyl green-check cloth. And the cottage's focal point, the vines, still hung low and luxuriant from the grooved, thick glass roof. It was amazing! Everything was exactly as it had always been, as though time had never interfered. And even this early in June, those same vines were already beginning to show the first signs of the fruit that was to come.

Half-forgotten memories began to flood back into Carrie's mind. She had been seven-years-old when she had first been brought here to be left in the care of her father's older half-sister, Aunt Lorna. Her parents had to go abroad on a business trip and it was only supposed to be a temporary arrangement.

3

They would be away for six months that was all, but tragedy stepped in.

In the end, Carrie had remained at Dell Cottage throughout her childhood, until she left for university, in fact, and, afterwards, moving North to begin her career. She then came back only for short and infrequent visits. That is, until Aunt Lorna became ill then Carrie had come home to look after her in those final days and weeks.

Dear Aunt Lorna—she had been a strange, solitary woman who, Carrie always thought, had very little time for children but a great deal of it for her precious garden. It had been her life and soul! Everywhere there were fruit trees, and flowers, planted for the bees. Herbs filled every corner, and in the winter, Carrie was remembering, there was utter silence.

The summer was entirely different. Always there were the songs of birds and the quiet, gentle gurgling of the river. Carrie smiled to herself. Yes, it was a restful place, but when one is seven-years-old, rest is neither appreciated nor required. And she was remembering now how she once asked if she could have a dog, and seeing again in her mind's eyes Aunt Lorna's sidelong glance.

'A dog,' she had repeated in a quiet tone. 'Why do you want a dog when there is so much nature to please you?'

'It would be my special friend. I think it would make me happy,' Carrie had replied.

Then her aunt had given her a strange smile, and her response had been even stranger.

'You're thinking again, dear,' she had said with a mysterious shake of the head. 'That won't do at all! And you don't need a dog, nor a special friend. Something else is waiting for you here.'

'What's waiting for me, Aunt Lorna?' Carrie remembered asking, and had no doubt looked a little apprehensive, too, knowing she was forever being told not to waste time with silly questions and too much thinking. It was the kind of thing that usually brought a brisk rebuke.

However, that time, there had been no sharp response. Instead, Aunt Lorna had answered in that strange, unruffled way of hers.

'Wait and see.'

'But what is it, Aunt Lorna? How do you know it's waiting for me?'

'I know, because I've seen it in my crystal. Now stop bothering me with your questions. I have work to do.'

Her words had mystified young Carrie, and for many years to come she had tried to persuade her aunt to tell her more, but Aunt Lorna had always refused to expand, and apart from that one time, she had never mentioned the crystal again.

For all that, when the air crash had taken

away both of Carrie's parents, Aunt Lorna had done her duty to her half-brother and his wife by taking Carrie under her wing. And in spite of the fact that she was never able to show her affection to people as much as she could to her garden, Carrie knew her aunt had always done her best.

With a small sigh now, Carrie turned away and made her way round to the front door. After opening it and stepping through into the entrance hall she paused, suddenly aware that she was shivering slightly. The cottage had been closed up for months, since the day after Aunt Lorna's funeral, in fact, and Carrie, duty done, had returned to her life up North. No-one had been living in it since and, she decided, it was probably the dampness that was making everywhere seem chilly, plus a little of her own tiredness, too. But, instinctively, she knew it was something more than that. It was that familiar sense of mysteriousness that had always surrounded her here.

Carrie's scalp began to tingle, just like it did at work when she was about to discover a new angle on something, a sure sign that something was about to happen. But then, throwing off the feeling as nothing more sinister than travel-weariness, she slipped off her jacket and tossed it across the banister at the foot of the stairs.

Wandering from room to room, Carrie found that very little had changed, and after collecting her suitcases from the car and setting her few necessary provisions down on to the kitchen table, she glanced along the window-ledge, vaguely surprised to see the usual row of Aunt Lorna's beloved herb pots still sitting there. She pressed her fingers into the soil, surprised to find it still moist. Vaguely, Carrie wondered who could have been in the cottage to water them. She wasn't aware that someone else had access to a key.

With a shrug she dismissed such thoughts, for the moment, at least! Instead, she gazed out of the kitchen window at the view beyond. The gap in the fence had still not been repaired. It had been her own private gap which she could squeeze through whenever Aunt Lorna's back was turned. And beyond the broken fence stretched the long slope of meadow-land that she had often roamed. It was studded by tall trees and beyond them lay the river, where for no reason at all except that it was somewhere to aim for, Carrie used to go, making for the water's edge and sitting down on the bank to daydream for hours until her aunt would call her in.

She turned away and filled the kettle, wondering what had happened to her old friends in the village. Were they still around, or had they, like herself, moved on? Natalie, for instance, her very best friend, who would sometimes meet her by the river where they would gather armfuls of wild flowers for their teacher. Natalie Woodward, like herself, was almost thirty now and Carrie hadn't seen her since the day of Aunt Lorna's funeral. Carrie found herself remembering them as children, Natalie's proud, young face, with its slanting green eyes and her erect carriage. Her nose had been as small as a button and, unlike Carrie's hair, which was light blonde, Natalie's was as red as flame and thickly curled, and always swatched up with bright ribbons. A long-forgotten rhyme suddenly came into her head, one that Natalie used to sing, 'Let him go, let him tarry, We'll all marry, except Carrie'.

Well, Carrie accepted, her friend had been right about that at least! Carrie had never married! She'd never met the right man, although for a time she believed she had found him in Declan. And there had been a few others before him, of course, some quite serious, but never serious enough for her to make any long-standing commitment. She wondered if Natalie had married in the time between, and if she had, to whom?

Carrie sighed. It had been a long drive down from Manchester and she was feeling more than a little weary. She heard the kettle switch itself off and she looked forward to a cup of tea. Reaching into one of the plastic carrier bags to take out a carton of milk and a packet of tea bags, she stooped to open the door of the fridge. Another surprise! Fresh milk was already waiting for her, standing next to a carton of eggs. On the shelf below was a pack of bacon rashers, together with a small brown loaf and two tubs of strawberry yoghurt.

Wide-eyed, Carrie stared down at them. Had someone been expecting her arrival? Completely puzzled, Carrie reached up to take a mug from the cupboard, deciding to investigate the mystery when she had had her cup of tea. But then, all thoughts of a mysterious benefactor disappeared as she heard someone rapping at the door. She turned quickly, recognising a vaguely familiar voice.

'Carrie! It's Natalie! May I come in?'

'Natalie!' she called back. 'Please do! The door's open!'

A tall, smiling, young woman came bursting through the door. The bright red hair had lost none of its colour, but the baggy yellow sweater over the brightly-striped pants barely disguised the extra pounds that just one short year can collect. Carrie smiled inwardly. Seeing her friend again reminded her of a rainbow. Natalie had always been artistic and had no real dress sense. In fact, her choice of colours left a lot to be desired!

For several minutes the two friends greeted one another, and when the joy of the reunion had all but abated, they wandered into the conservatory with their tea mugs and sat down together at the table.

'You don't look a day older, Carrie,' Natalie

observed once they'd settled, her sharp eyes taking in Carrie's slim figure, her thick fair hair and brown eyes.

'But it is only a year since we last saw each other, Nat!'

'I know, but you're still as gorgeous as ever! And so slim! How do you do it? It's simply not fair! You always did make me feel like a dinosaur.'

Carrie laughed.

'What nonsense!' she replied. 'But thanks for the compliment, anyway. And thanks, too, for the milk and eggs. Not only was it very thoughtful of you, but you've solved my mystery for me.'

'What mystery? What milk and eggs?'

'The ones I've found in the fridge. You put them there, didn't you?'

'Not me! I don't know anything about them.'

'Then who else could it have been? Who else has a key? Do you know?'

'Perhaps it's the agent chap, the man who's been keeping an eye on the place for you. Why don't you ask him?'

'I will,' Carrie confirmed, nodding her head. 'I suppose it must be him, although he didn't say anything about it when I called in his office a little while ago.'

Natalie giggled.

'Perhaps it's Aunt Lorna coming back to keep an eye on you. You know what an odd girl she was.'

Carrie shook her head, puzzled.

'Well, odd or not, I can't see my aunt coming back to haunt me with milk and eggs.'

They both laughed, then she regarded Natalie Woodward with affection.

'Well, no doubt I'll solve the mystery in time. Now let's talk about you. Tell me, what have you been up to these last few years? Let's face it, neither of us has been any great shakes in the letter-writing department, have we?'

Natalie gave a rueful shrug.

'That's true,' she admitted, 'but, to be quite honest, I've never had that much to tell you. As you know, I'm still living in the village, still in the same house, footloose and fancy-free, and, oh, yes, I managed to land that job I wanted.'

'The teaching job at our old school?' Carrie asked and when Natalie grinned and nodded, Carrie added delightedly, 'Good for you, Nat! I know that's what you set your heart on. What are you teaching?'

'Oh, all sorts of things! But I suppose you could say that drama and music are my pets. I'm very involved with both of them, inside school hours and out. I've actually organised a choir, too—well, more a singing group really—and it's not only for the children but for the grown-ups, too.'

'Sounds good. Is it a success?'

'Yes, very much so. It's really doing well. We

put on a show now and then, although I doubt we'd ever challenge Sir Andrew Lloyd Webber or the West End. But we're not too bad as amateurs go. We're doing West Side Story next. We're in the middle of rehearsals right now.' Clearly, a thought struck her and she added, 'You'll have to consider joining us.'

'With my voice? No way. You know I can't sing—or dance—for toffee!'

'Well, we can always use help in other ways, you know.'

'Well, we'll see. Let me settle in first.'

'Of course. What are your plans, by the way?'

Carrie shrugged then replied, 'I'm not quite sure.'

'Will you be staying here for good now that Aunt Lorna's left you this cottage? Will you still keep on writing your articles and things? It's a long way from the big city if you intend to carry on with your magazine job.'

Carrie nodded.

'Yes, I do know, but, fortunately, I have no pressing problems to earn any money at the moment. Aunt Lorna's been very generous, and, besides, I'd half decided to give up my job when I came back here to look after her. Now, so much has happened since, let's say I'm taking a sabbatical. I suppose I can always freelance if things get tight. But, to be honest, Nat, I would like a complete change. Things haven't been going so well lately.'

'Man trouble?'

'In a way, but I'd got myself in a bit of a rut anyway. Sometimes you need something like this to push you off in another direction.'

'That's true! But this chap of yours—Declan, was it—wasn't he an actor, or something?'

'He wasn't my Declan! But, yes, he was something of an actor, in more ways than one!'

Carrie frowned, remembering Declan's handsome face, the male-model features and his air of total confidence. But she was remembering, too, his lack of depth, his vanity and his constant lies. Hot anger suddenly washed over her as she remembered how much time she had wasted on him.

Natalie, spotting Carrie's flash of rage, knew she'd touched a nerve.

'Oops! Sorry!' she apologised quickly. 'I'll drop the subject, shall I?'

'Thanks! I'd be grateful.'

'OK. So, going back to your career, you'll have to take over Aunt Lorna's line of business.'

Carrie looked across sharply.

'Do you mean the herbs?'

'Why not? She seemed to do very well with them.'

Carrie frowned slightly.

'And get labelled a witch, as she was?'

'Oh, that's a bit strong, Carrie.'

'Perhaps it is, but I remember what people

used to say about her.'

Carrie's eyes darkened again. Like all children, she had wanted normality and she had often been embarrassed by her aunt's quixotic ways, her strange eccentricities. And even more so when people would come to the cottage to have their horoscopes read, or buy her herbal remedies and then, afterwards, to see her take their money and stow it away in a copper pot.

However, moments later, she glanced across at Natalie, her face clearing and her good humour returning.

'Anyway, she always said I didn't have the gift.'

Natalie gave a careless shrug.

'Oh, well, something will turn up no doubt.'

Carrie nodded, taking a sip of her tea.

'So,' she asked, 'how's everyone in the village? Has it changed much?'

'Not a great deal. There are a few incomers on the new estate, and the old Danyderi house has been done up.'

Carrie's head jerked in surprised.

'Danyderi? Who'd be mad enough to buy that broken-down horror?'

Natalie's eyes twinkled.

'A rather dishy chap from London, as a matter of fact. We're all after his attention.'

Carrie grinned.

'Any luck?'

'Not so far. But I'm hoping to persuade him

14

to join my drama group. We're rather short of good-looking men, and he's certainly that.'

'What's he doing with Danyderi? It's a bit off the beaten track, isn't it? No-one's lived in it for years. It'll cost a fortune to make it even habitable.'

Natalie nodded.

'Yes, I know, and no-one's quite sure what he's doing there. He doesn't mix much. His name is James Alexander and I believe he's a pilot or something. Apparently he stays in his flat in London when he's not off around the world, so he doesn't get down here very often, which is a shame, really. He's certainly the best-looking male that's been seen around here, I can vouch for that.'

Carrie smiled. Natalie had always been something of a romantic.

'Oh, well, maybe I'll get to meet this wondrous creature one day but, knowing my luck, I won't hold my breath. Now tell me about the others. What about Jean and Kathryn, and Josie? Tell me how they all are.'

Carrie couldn't be sure, but for a brief moment, Natalie's expression seemed to change and her lively eyes momentarily darkened. But the change was so fleeting that Carrie wondered if she had imagined it.

'Jean and Kathryn are still here,' Natalie began. 'They're both married now, but of course you knew that.'

When Carrie nodded that she did, Natalie

15

went on.

'In fact, Jean's and David's little girl is one of my pupils.'

'And Josie?'

There was another brief pause, and Carrie saw again that momentary withdrawal on Natalie's face.

'I can't really say how Josie is,' she replied.

'Oh? Why not? Has she moved away?'

Natalie seemed uncomfortable. However, after yet another, even briefer, pause she shrugged slightly and went on, 'She just isn't around anymore. No-one knows where she is.'

Carrie threw her a quick glance, aware of something in Natalie's tone.

'Isn't around? What do you mean?' she asked.

Natalie shook her head.

'Just that! She isn't here anymore.'

'So, where is she?'

'Nobody knows. She just went! One day she was here, and the next day she wasn't!'

'How very strange.'

Carrie was puzzled to hear such news about Josie Barnes. She had been a quiet girl, sometimes too quiet, but she had always found her to be a kind and gentle girl, and certainly not the type who would leave everything behind without good reason.

'Hasn't she been in touch with anyone?'

'No. Not a word to a soul.'

'How strange,' Carrie repeated. 'And when

16

was all this? How long is it since anyone's seen her?'

Natalie gave a slight shrug.

'Not very long, about three months I would say. She simply went off one morning and never came back.'

'How very strange,' Carrie repeated.

'At first we were all quite concerned, still are, to be honest. Her father checked that she wasn't with any of her family or friends, in fact we all did. And then he contacted the police, but because she's not a child there wasn't very much they could do except put her on a missing persons' list.'

'It all seems very odd indeed, not like Josie at all.'

Natalie gave another brief nod.

'I agree, and there have been no reports of any accidents either because, naturally, that was all checked out.'

'Well, I suppose that's a good sign. Perhaps it's Josie's choice that she's gone away. Perhaps we're reading too much into it. I mean, she is over twenty-one, isn't she? Why shouldn't she go away if she wants to?'

'No reason at all,' Natalie replied but she looked doubtful. 'But you don't really believe that, do you, Carrie? Of all of us, Josie is the least likely to do anything so unpredictable.'

Carrie had to agree.

'You say this happened about three months ago?' she asked, and when Natalie nodded

17

that it was, Carrie rose to her feet, gathering up the two mugs and taking them into the kitchen.

For some strange reason she found she was suddenly shaking. Natalie followed her and stood quietly in the doorway as Carrie rinsed the mugs.

'Well,' Carrie said softly, 'I hope she's OK, wherever she is. Josie was a really nice girl.'

She shivered. Why was she speaking in the past tense? She placed the mugs on to the draining tray before turning back to Natalie.

'I think after that we both need cheering up. Would you like some more tea? I can soon make a fresh cup.'

But Natalie shook her head.

'No, thanks, Carrie. I must get off. I only called in to welcome you back.'

'Well, I'm glad you did,' Carrie replied, drying her hands on a teacloth, 'in spite of your news about Josie. It's really nice to see you again.'

She walked with Natalie to the front door and the two girls embraced each other once again.

'Don't forget to think about joining our drama group, will you?' Natalie reminded her as she opened the door of her car. 'Willing hands are always welcome. And I'll fix up a get-together with the girls, supper or something, at my place. I know they're all looking forward to seeing you again.'

'Sounds good! And I won't forget to give the drama group some thought, either,' Carrie promised.

'Right! I'll be in touch.'

As her friend drove off with a final wave, Carrie, still shaking, went back indoors.

Later, however, upstairs in her old room, unpacking her suitcases, she was suddenly gripped by a feeling of dread. She sat down quickly on the edge of the bed, her hands clenching into taut, white-knuckled balls as unwelcome images began to swim around in her mind, and sounds, too, of rushing water, voices raised against the wind, gravel crunching, and the sloping zigzag of a high cliff.

What was the matter with her? Then, through the confusion came yet another sound. A bell was ringing somewhere, and it took Carrie several moments to realise that it was coming from her own front door.

'Oh, thank goodness,' she cried, rushing down the stairs and wrenching open the door. 'Natalie, have you forgotten something?'

But she stopped suddenly when she saw that it wasn't Natalie standing in the doorway. It was the tall figure of a man, and a very good-looking man at that! He stood on the doorstep, his dark eyes looking candidly down at Carrie. His shoulders were broad and his back was straight, and his voice when he spoke, was deep and pleasant.

'Hi! I think these belong to you.'

19

CHAPTER TWO

Carrie looked blankly at the stranger on the doorstep of the cottage. She was completely at a loss.

'I'm—I'm sorry?' she stammered.

The man held up a set of keys, jingling them like a bell.

'I believe these are yours.'

She gave him a mystified look.

'No, they're not mine. I have my own keys.'

He smiled patiently.

'Yes, I know you have, but these are the spare set.'

'Spare set?' Carrie repeated lamely. 'But where did you get them from?'

'From Lorna, of course. I've been looking after things until—'

He paused, aware of Carrie's growing confusion.

'Look,' he said, his smile fading and a look of apology taking its place, 'perhaps I'd better explain.'

'Yes, I think perhaps you had.'

'Well, you see, I was a friend of your aunt's and I—'

He paused again, uncertainly.

'I have a feeling that I've given you a bit of a shock.'

'Well, yes,' Carrie replied.

'I assure you I didn't mean to. I just came by to return your cottage keys and to see if there was anything else you needed. You'd better take them.'

Robot-like, Carrie accepted the bunch of keys which he was now pressing into her hand.

'I'm sorry,' she said, finally finding her voice, 'you said to see if there was anything else I needed. What do you mean exactly?'

The man, clearly embarrassed, now gave a small, crooked smile.

'I think perhaps I should have phoned first. I've obviously caught you off-balance and that was far from my intention. Please, my name is Alexander, James Alexander,' he added, extending his hand.

'Carrie Davies,' she answered automatically and shook his hand.

Although still very bewildered, the man's easy-going manner was beginning to make Carrie feel more composed.

'And no,' she assured him, her tone more even now, 'you haven't caught me off-balance, well, at least, not very much. It's just that I didn't expect anyone.'

'I can see that, and again I apologise.'

She managed a smile.

'There's no need, and I'm not being very neighbourly, am I? Won't you come in?'

'Well, if you're sure.'

As Carrie opened the door a little wider, James stepped through into the hallway before following her along the short passageway into the living-room. She opened a bookcase drawer and tossed in the keys, while he stood a little awkwardly in the centre of the room.

From the moment Carrie had opened the door to him, James had recognised her from the photograph. He'd often glanced at the girl in the silver frame sitting on Lorna's mantelpiece, and had felt a distinct attraction. There had been something about her that appealed to him, but he could never quite say what it was, until now.

James was sensing something in her that was hard to define, a sort of mixture of pride and self-assurance that mingled somehow with a wary sensitivity. Yes, it was all there. But he was picking up something else about her, too, an extra something. There was an openness about her, a distinct honesty, and, instinctively, James felt that Carrie Davies would be the kind of girl with whom he would never have to put on any sort of act.

She turned towards him and, with a broad sweep of her hand, invited him to take a seat. And as he did so she, in her turn, assessed James Alexander.

'Was it you who put the milk and eggs into my fridge?' she asked.

'Yes. I hope you didn't mind.'

Carrie sat down opposite him.

'No, not at all, it was very thoughtful of you, although I did bring some emergency rations with me.'

'Ah, but I'll bet you forgot the bacon.'

'I rarely eat it.'

And as she listened to James Alexander's pleasant voice telling her that, for him at least, there was nothing better than a plate of bacon and eggs to start the day, Carrie confirmed that Natalie's description of her neighbour was, indeed, accurate. He seemed to be making himself very much at home, relaxing in the chair with his long legs stretched out before him. And he suited the light tan slacks he wore, too, and the brown short-sleeved shirt. He had nice, even teeth and, close up, he was even more attractive than Carrie had first thought, with deep brown eyes that reminded her of chocolate, and which were studying her now with as much curiosity as her own was of him.

'I take it then,' she heard herself saying, 'that you knew Aunt Lorna well.'

'Yes, quite well. She was an interesting old girl.'

On his frequent visits to the village of Tyr Gwyn, James had, indeed, got to know Lorna Davies, and had grown very fond of her, too. He was sorry when he'd learned of her rather sudden death, and regretted that he hadn't been able to attend her funeral. He had been in Kuala Lumpur when the news had reached him, and all he'd been able to do for his old friend and neighbour was to wire her some

23

flowers.

He regarded Carrie. This was the first time he had actually come face to face with Lorna's niece, although she had spoken of her often enough. And he was glad he'd decided to bring the keys back himself, in spite of the initial confusion, instead of leaving them with the agent as he'd originally intended to do.

'Would you like some tea?' he heard Carrie ask. 'Or a beer, perhaps?'

'No, thanks, I'm fine.'

There was a moment's pause then, her curiosity aroused, Carrie asked, 'Why did my aunt give you the spare keys? How well did you know her?'

He looked surprised.

'Didn't she tell you about me?'

'No.'

'That surprises me.'

'Does it? Why?'

He shrugged, and his mouth quirked into a half smile.

'I'm vain enough to think she might have mentioned me, even if it was only to tell you what an excellent neighbour I was.'

Carrie smiled, too. His humour was contagious.

'Well, I'm sorry to disappoint you but she didn't. In fact, I didn't know you existed until today.'

'That's not very flattering.'

'I'm sorry, I didn't mean it to sound rude.

But tell me, how did you meet my aunt?'

He straightened up, pulling in his long legs.

'I met her about . . . let me see . . . it must be around five years ago now.'

'As long ago as that?'

'Yes, it must be. I'd come down here on leave one time, to stay with a friend of mine, Steve Butler. Do you know him?'

Carrie did. He was one of the boys from the village. When she nodded, James went on.

'We were at university together. We're good friends and it was while I was spending a few days' leave with him that I bumped into Lorna.'

Carrie smiled wryly.

'Bumped?'

James shrugged again, even more good-humouredly.

'Metaphorically speaking, of course. I was driving back from Cardiff when I spotted her on the Trefwr road. She was standing on the grass verge looking quite lost and forlorn. I remember thinking that the clapped-out old banger she had been driving must have been almost as old as she was. Quite ungallant of me, I admit.' He gave a small, apologetic shrug.

'Anyway,' he went on, 'the car had obviously broken down, and I, being the very essence of a gentleman who hates to see ladies in distress, pulled up and offered my services. It turned out she had a flat, so I changed the tyre.'

'I see.'

'And while I was doing my good deed, we started chatting. She told me she lived here at Dell Cottage, and wondered if I knew it. I said I'd heard of it, and wasn't she the lady who was an expert in herbal cures? She told me she was and then, I remember, she gave me quite a long lecture on the beneficial properties of various plants.'

'I see,' Carrie murmured again.

'After I'd fixed the tyre, I offered to drive behind her to make sure the car held out.'

'And she agreed, I take it.'

'Yes, of course. The next day,' he continued, 'I rang her to see if she was OK and she invited me round for a thank-you drink which, rather disappointingly, turned out to be a glass of herbal tea accompanied by another commentary on the rudiments of alternative medicine.'

Carrie pulled a face and he threw her a brief grin.

'It was quite interesting actually. She almost converted me. Anyway, after that we got on like a house on fire.'

'Quite a knight of the road, aren't you?' was Carrie's wry comment.

'I suppose you could say I was—or am. We kept in touch after that. I rang her quite a lot, keeping my eye on her, so to speak, and she would ring me. And whenever I came to Tyr Gwyn I made it my business to call on her although most of the time my solicitous spirit seemed to end up with me having to repair something or other for her—wobbly shelves, door hinges—you name it.'

Carrie laughed, and James liked the sound of it.

'Typical Aunt Lorna! She was very good at that!' Carrie chuckled. 'As a rule, she was immensely self-reliant but, if it suited her purpose, she could always find something for someone to do.'

'Now you're the one who's being ungallant. Anyway, I didn't mind. It made me feel quite useful really.'

'So useful that you decided to move here?'

He laughed, a deep, throaty chuckle.

'Not quite that, and not at first. I happened to mention to her that I was looking for somewhere away from London where I could spend my free time, a bolt-hole in the country, that kind of thing. I get so fed up with the rat-race. Anyway she put me on to Danyderi. It had just been put on the market and was going for a song. She said it would make a wonderful permanent home for me, away from all the pressures of my job. When I went to see it, although I could see it needed a lot of work, I had to agree that it had potential. I decided to buy it, and I'm glad I did. I think it was a very good move indeed.'

He grinned at Carrie, regarding her in silence for a few moments. Carrie flushed slightly.

'Are you sure you wouldn't like a beer or something?' she asked, aware that he was flirting with her and that she was quite enjoying it.

'Well,' he said, 'perhaps I will change my mind about that.'

'Not at all.'

Carrie rose and disappeared into the kitchen, glad of the excuse to take a breather from his far-too-attractive presence. A few moments later she returned with a can of beer, a glass, and another one containing orange juice. She handed him the beer and then moved back to her chair. After taking a sip of her juice she looked across at James again, aware that he'd been studying her every moment.

'So,' he said as he filled his glass, 'what about you? I think we've talked enough about me.'

'What about me?'

'Anything. Everything. Your plans for the future?'

And so, Carrie found herself telling him of the job she had just left, and a little of her life up North. It seemed that she was talking for a long time without any interruption from James. She noticed, too, that he was listening with extreme attentiveness and then, as her ramblings petered out, Carrie began to wonder if perhaps she'd talked a little too much.

'Look,' she said with a slight frown, 'thank you for bringing back the keys and for the bacon and stuff, but perhaps I'm keeping you back.'

'No, you're not keeping me from anything. I've got all day.'

He almost added, to get to know you, but he didn't. Having only met, he didn't want to give the impression that he was rushing things.

Instead, he said, 'I'm perfectly free until seven o'clock tonight.'

Carrie took another sip of her juice and glanced at him again, asking casually, 'And what's happening at seven o'clock?'

He answered her with a brief smile.

'I've been volunteered to help out with the local musical and drama group. Can't sing a note, mind you, but I think they see me as a fairly good scene-shifter or something.'

Carrie grinned.

'You as well? Natalie was twisting my arm to join them just before you arrived.'

'And are you? Joining them, I mean?'

'I don't know yet. Probably.'

'Good!'

Carrie was flattered to note that James seemed so pleased, and she would have been more so if she had been able to read his thoughts, that her joining the group, too, would give him a marvellous excuse to see her on a regular basis, or as regularly as his job would allow.

'They're quite a good bunch,' Carrie went on briskly, not mentioning the fact that she liked the idea of seeing him on a regular basis, too. 'And they'll probably be a little short-handed since Josie's gone away.'

Was she mistaken, or did his manner change? Carrie couldn't be sure.

'You knew Josie then?' he asked quietly.

'Yes, I did.'

Now they were both referring to the girl in the past tense! Her scalp began to tingle again.

'Did—do you know her, too?'

James gave a brief nod of the head.

'Fairly well. Steve introduced me to her at one of his parties, and she's done a little part-time office-work for me. I remember thinking that they both seemed pretty close, too, although she didn't strike me as the type Steve usually went for.'

'What type was that?'

'He always went for the er—how can I describe it—more positive type,' he said, placing his now-empty beer glass on the table by his side. 'More outgoing. Josie came across to me as a quiet sort of girl.'

Carrie nodded her agreement.

'Yes, she was certainly that! Even when she was small she liked nothing better than to go off on her own somewhere and paint.'

'Paint?'

'Oh, yes! And very good she was, I mean, is, too. In fact, come to think of it, all my old

30

school chums are artistic and clever. Natalie has always loved her drama and singing. Jean's forever writing poetry—'

'And Josie painted.'

'Yes. I remember she won a prize once for a water-colour she did of the river by Ty Mynydd, where it curves round. It's the local beauty spot.'

'Yes, I know it.' James nodded slowly. 'That must have been the attraction between them.'

'What must?'

'Their mutual interest in painting. Steve was good at it, too, as I recall.'

'I see.' Carrie looked surprised. 'To be honest, I don't remember much about any of the boys we knew.'

She stopped suddenly as the phone rang.

'I'm sorry! Will you excuse me a moment? I didn't realise anyone knew I was home yet.'

Her caller was Natalie.

'Hi, Carrie! Look, I know you'll be up to your eyes in unpacking and things, but have you thought any more about joining our group?'

'Well, yes, and I probably will.'

'Oh, good! In that case, can you get over here by seven o'clock this evening?'

'Well, I hadn't bargained on coming tonight. I've still got lots to do.'

'Carrie, you must! We're really short. Please say you will. We'd all be most grateful for a helping hand.'

'Well, I . . .'

Carrie paused, frowning thoughtfully for a moment before glancing through the open doorway at James who was flipping through the pages of a magazine. She made up her mind.

'OK, Natalie,' she answered brightly. 'Why not? The unpacking can wait.'

'Brilliant! See you at seven in the old school hall.'

Then Carrie heard the click as she rang off. James glanced up as she went back into the sitting-room.

'Everything all right?' he asked.

Carrie nodded.

'Yes, fine. It was Natalie. They're short-handed, apparently and, like you, I've just volunteered my services to West Side Story.'

'Excellent!' he exclaimed, rising to his feet.

Carrie rose, too.

'I'll see you to the door.'

And, for a moment, as his hand brushed against hers in the doorway, something reached out between them and touched them, and Carrie felt her heart bump. She felt certain that he was aware of this something, too, for his face changed as he looked down at her. He seemed about to say something and then changed his mind.

With a murmured, 'I'll see you later then,' he was gone.

CHAPTER THREE

Tr Gwyn was a close-knit village with the placid River Dulas flowing at its feet. It lay snugly between the river and the steep grassy slopes of Ty Mynydd, the high, pointed mountain which gave the place its name, and towered like a sentinel to all that lay in its shadow. It was a small community where very little went on without everybody else knowing about it, too.

It was later that evening, at precisely seven o'clock, when Carrie drove through the gates of the local junior school and parked her car. The lights in the school were already ablaze, and as Carrie crossed the playground towards the main entrance, she could hear lively bursts of singing coming from within. She paused momentarily as she reached the door, her hand on the brass handle and a small, nervous smile playing around her lips. Clearly, the rehearsal for the Tyr Gwyn Drama and Musical Society's latest production was already well under way.

Almost gingerly, she pushed open the door and made her way along the chalk-smelling corridor which led into the main assembly hall. As she entered, two dozen pairs of eyes turned towards her, and the singing and the laughter immediately subsided into a curious silence.

Carrie stood in the doorway, her smile uneasy and not knowing quite what to do. But then, suddenly, her discomfort was dispelled by loud hoots of recognition and soon she was being smothered by many warm hugs of welcome.

'Here, take a seat, Carrie, and grab one of these!'

Someone thrust a musical score into her hand, and someone else passed her a chair. With a nod of encouragement from Natalie, and barely having time to catch her breath, Carrie was soon joining in the chorus of a rendition of one of her favourite numbers from the show! But, even though she was singing as heartily as the rest of them, she soon found that her eyes were constantly drawn to the door as it opened to admit yet another late arrival. When the one she was looking out for finally made his appearance, Carrie's heart gave an unexpected leap.

However, her excitement faded when she saw that James was not alone. A tall, dark-haired girl preceded him, and although he gave Carrie a small, salutary wave of recognition, his manner towards the girl made Carrie wonder how close the two of them were. She watched as he guided the girl to the other side of the room, his hand lightly touching her elbow, and as he pulled up two chairs, Carrie noticed how closely he placed them together.

She came quickly back to earth, and for

some absurd reason she felt very annoyed with herself. The man had every right to be with any girl if he wished! It had nothing to do with her! Still irritated with herself, she deliberately forced her attention back to the matter in hand, the show.

The rehearsal continued, and later, when the singing had subsided, she heard a voice say quietly in her ear, 'We were all so sorry about Aunt Lorna.'

Carrie, with a start, glanced up from the music to find herself looking into the smiling face of her old friend, Jean Owen. Jean, whose easy-going friendliness made her popular wherever she went, pulled up another chair and sat down beside Carrie, planting a chaste kiss on Carrie's cheek.

'But, as they say, every cloud has its silver lining and at least it's brought you back amongst us,' she said sweetly.

'Thank you, Jean,' Carrie replied, returning the smile. 'It's good to see you again.'

'It's so good to see you again, too,' Jean responded in her cheerful way. 'Natalie rang me earlier and told me you were back at Dell Cottage and that she hoped to persuade you to come and join us tonight.'

Carrie smiled.

'Yes, Nat's very persuasive. How's David? Is he with you?'

'He's fine, but he's not here tonight. It's his turn to baby-sit.'

Carrie regarded Jean as they chatted on. Always capable, Jean had a strong, no-nonsense manner. She and David Owen had been sweethearts since their schooldays and when they got married at the ripe old age of eighteen, no-one in Tyr Gwyn had been the least bit surprised.

'Natalie's a bully,' Jean was chatting on. 'She press-gangs all of us but nobody seems to mind. We all know she's doing a great job with her drama group. The children love her. And she's so keen to get this show off to a good start that she's roping in the entire village, especially now she's short of a very important member of the cast.'

'You mean Josie?'

'Yes, did Nat tell you about her?'

'Yes, she did. It all seems to be a bit of a mystery, doesn't it?'

'It certainly does.'

'Where do you think she is, Jean?'

'Like everyone else, I've no idea. There are plenty of rumours flying round though!'

'Such as?'

'Well, some say she's met some chap in London and has gone off with him, but I can't really believe that. Others say she's decided to go away on holiday and forgot to mention the fact, but I believe that even less. No-one knows for sure.'

'Did she ever mention that she'd met someone? Or that she was thinking of going away on holiday?'

'Not a word! And I for one didn't get the impression she had any intentions of going away, either on holiday or to meet some guy. Quite the reverse! When she knew for sure that she'd been chosen to play the lead in West Side Story she was very excited about it. She was a bit nervous, of course, who wouldn't be? But not nervous enough to be scared away.'

Carrie threw her a quick glance.

'You say scared, Jean. What makes you think she was scared?'

Jean pulled a face.

'Did I say scared? I don't know why I said that. Maybe it was her attitude of late, very jumpy. But you know how edgy Josie has always been about things.'

'Well, yes, edgy, but you said scared.'

Jean shook her head.

'Well, I don't know why I did. Bad choice of word.'

There was a moment's uneasy pause and the two girls turned to watch Natalie direct the rehearsal. There was something far too worrying about the fact that Josie Barnes had been so long absent from Tyr Gwyn, and without saying a word to anyone. Someone must know something! As Carrie listened to the singers going through their solos, her feelings were a complex mixture of doubt and concern.

'Right, everyone!'

37

Natalie was calling out to them all, clapping her hands together in order to gain their attention and get them all in their places for the scene she was about to rehearse. As Carrie watched Natalie, who was clearly loving every minute of the rehearsal, she tried to force her attention back to the show. As people took their places she recognised two of the men who were obviously playing leading roles. As she watched them go through their routines, Carrie tried hard to quash her concern about Josie, not to mention her disappointment about James Alexander, and concentrated on the figures up on the stage.

But it wasn't long before her eyes turned once more to James. He was sitting alone now. His companion had gone up on to the stage. Carrie could see her standing by the piano with Natalie. Another girl was with them, and all three seemed to be discussing something in the script, and James's companion, Carrie noted, wasn't looking too happy about things.

Carrie turned back to James and, as she did so, flushed slightly to find his eyes on her. He smiled and winked and then, when one of the men sat down beside him and he looked away, Carrie turned back to Jean, her thoughts flitting back to Josie Barnes.

'When was the last time you saw Josie? Can you remember?' she asked Jean.

Jean frowned thoughtfully and pursed her lips.

'Let me see,' she murmured. 'It would be a couple of days before she went off. Yes, I remember. It was on the Monday evening. We'd all gone round to Nat's to have a chat about the show.'

'And how did she seem?'

'Just as usual, I think,' Jean answered. 'We talked mainly about the cast list as I recall and she seemed fine about playing Maria.'

'Who else was there?'

Jean frowned again.

'Well, there was Nat and Josie, of course, and myself, and then there was Kathryn and Jenny, and Jenny's sister, Joanna. And a couple of others who haven't lived in the village for very long so I don't think you'd know them.'

She glanced across at the stage.

'There's one of them now,' she pointed out, 'the tall, dark-haired girl who came in with that gorgeous chap sitting over there. Her name is Adele Parry and he's James Alexander. He's moved into Danyderi, by the way. Isn't he a dish? I'll introduce you later.'

'No need to, Jean,' Carrie murmured. 'We've already met.'

Jean turned to her in surprise.

'Really? How?'

'He's been looking after Dell Cottage for Aunt Lorna and he brought over a set of spare keys not long after I'd arrived.'

'I see. Now I come to think of it, your aunt

and he did become quite friendly.'

'It would seem so.'

'Anyway, where was I? Oh, yes, our Miss Parry. She's from Devon, I believe, although from all accounts, she says her family is originally from round these parts although no-one seems to remember them. She came to Tyr Gwyn about six months ago to work at the hospital at Trefwr. Said she was following in her father's footsteps as he was a doctor there once.'

Jean studied the girl for a few moments more then pulled a somewhat rueful face.

'Pretty, isn't she? The local lads are queueing up at her door. She's playing one of the smaller parts, but I wouldn't be surprised if Nat doesn't offer her Maria now that Josie's done a bunk. Not only is she very pretty, but she has a sweet voice.'

Carrie's eyes followed Jean's gaze. Adele Parry was certainly good-looking, and Carrie could well imagine the impact she would have on any vain and vulnerable male. She was tall and graceful, and had a very attractive smile and a confident manner. Perhaps a little over-confident, Carrie thought somewhat uncharitably.

'And the man who's playing opposite her, one of the Puerto Ricans? I seem to remember him, he looks familiar.'

'Of course he looks familiar. It's Steve Butler, remember? He was in our class at school. Surely you remember his little sister, Megan. The little girl who drowned all those years ago.'

Carrie gasped. Of course, she remembered! The whole village had been distraught when Steve's father and uncle had found the little three-year-old in the river that day at Ty Mynydd. The tragedy had stayed with all of them for months! Still did. And no-one had ever discovered why a child so young had wandered off so far. It had been a disaster that had pretty well broken all their hearts, not only the Butler family, but the whole of Tyr Gwyn as well.

The piano started up again, along with more of the singing, and the two girls fell silent for a while. Natalie, eyes bright, was directing the dancing scene of the two rival gangs as they headed for the fight, and was yelling hoarsely now in an attempt to make herself understood.

'Remember, you are in New York now and not in a little Welsh village! Be aggressive! Look angry!'

Much later, as the rehearsal drew to a close, Carrie suddenly found James standing close behind her. She turned to him, a little shaken by the way his eyes were looking down at her.

'We're all off down to the pub,' he said quietly. 'Will you join us?'

'Well,' she answered after a moment's thought, 'I hadn't planned on it. I still have lots to do at home.'

'It'll wait for you.'

Carrie laughed.

'Yes, it'll certainly do that. OK! Why not? Which pub?'

'The White Hart.'

'Right! I'll see you down there.'

Some fifteen minutes later, Carrie threaded her way through the crowded little bar and joined the more thirsty members of the cast in the lounge, where everyone seemed to be talking at once. And as soon as he saw Carrie heading for their table, James stood up and offered her his chair, dragging another one over for himself, turning it round and sitting across it straggle-legged.

Thanking him, Carrie sat down and looked around the crowded bar. She was recognising most of the faces now, faces once so familiar in her childhood, now perhaps a little older and rounder from the years between. There was no sign of Adele Parry, she noted, although most of those who had been at the rehearsal had arrived. They were soon all caught up in some light-hearted teasing about the casting.

'Now now, my children,' Natalie broke in, 'let's not have any squabbling in the cast.'

'Any ideas who's to take the part of Maria?' Jean asked no-one in particular, 'assuming, that is, that Josie doesn't come back.'

A small hush fell over them and all eyes turned to Natalie.

'Well,' she answered slowly, 'we'll have to

decide soon. We can't wait much longer to see if Jo will come back. We are running out of time as it is.'

She glanced at the faces around her as if waiting for suggestions, and when none came she added quietly, 'I was thinking that Adele might—'

'Oh, she will!' Gaynor Edwards interrupted, a short, brown-haired girl whom Carrie recognised as the school swot. 'In fact, I should say she's counting on it, wouldn't you?'

There was a murmur of mutual agreement and in the following few moments of discussion, Carrie watched them all with interest. She was definitely picking up a feeling from the majority that Adele, although unanimously accepted as suitable for the part of the leading lady, was not at the top of their popularity pole.

'Has anyone mentioned it to her yet?' James asked, entering into the discussion for the first time.

'Yes, I brought it up with her earlier tonight,' Natalie responded. 'I think she'd quite like the challenge. No-one can argue that she hasn't got the voice for it, and the looks.'

'That's true enough,' Mark Jones agreed, turning with a grin to Steve Butler, who was sitting a little away from the rest of them. 'What do you say, Steve? I'll bet your mate, Ian, rather fancies the idea of playing her lover-boy, even though it's only on stage.'

Steve glanced across, not much interest showing on his lean, hard face.

'Why should he?' he shrugged. 'It's only a show.'

'Really, Steve,' Natalie admonished, 'that's not the attitude at all! We'd all appreciate a little more interest, if you don't mind. After all, if Ian and Adele are to play the star-crossed Maria and Tony and don't take their roles seriously then it could all turn out to be quite a disaster. Remember, the whole show depends upon them being believable.'

She looked around the busy bar.

'Where are they both, by the way?'

No-one seemed to know and, when the glasses were emptied, one by one, with promises to meet again for the next rehearsal, they all began to take their leave.

'Would you like me to see you home?' James asked, rising from his chair to help Carrie on with her jacket.

'Not at all,' she answered quickly. 'I have my car, but thanks anyway.'

'Don't mention it. I just wanted to play knight of the road again.'

And with a mischievous grin he escorted her out of the pub and walked with her across the carpark.

'You'll find my telephone number in Lorna's desk,' he told her as she got into her car. 'Don't forget to ring me if you need a hand with anything.'

44

Carrie looked up and smiled.

'I won't. And thanks again. Good-night!'

'Good-night!'

In her rear-view mirror, Carrie could see that he was still watching her as she drove away. Back at Dell Cottage, she glanced down at the two suitcases sitting in the hall. It was almost eleven o'clock, far too late to bother with the rest of her unpacking tonight, and in any case she really couldn't be bothered. So, deciding to leave it until morning when the rest of her bits and pieces were due to arrive, she went into the kitchen and made herself a hot chocolate. A short time later, after a quick shower and with the tunes from the show still ringing in her head, she went upstairs to bed.

Lying there, subconsciously she thought of James and felt her skin tingle. He was far too attractive a man to have around too often, especially if his intentions were otherwise directed. Carrie sighed. Wasn't it just her rotten luck that he'd already met someone else? Oh, well. She snuggled down and closed her eyes. It had been a very long day and she was ready for a very long sleep.

But then the atmosphere suddenly changed, and the sensation of strangeness was returning. Carrie's eyes had barely closed in sleep when images rushed back into her head, images like earlier in her room. The sounds came again, those same distorted, disturbing sounds, and rushing water, too. And there were voices, and two indistinct and wind-tossed figures struggling on a cliff face.

Suddenly afraid, Carrie swallowed hard and tried to sit up, but found she couldn't. It was as though something was lying heavy on her chest, like a stone, and she could neither move a limb nor open her eyes. Her breath was rasping and her face felt wet and cold. And, soon, there was darkness everywhere.

How long she lay there, Carrie did not know, as though almost thankful for the shelter of the night. But then, with a jerk she blinked open her eyes, reaching across to switch on the bedside lamp. As her mind adjusted to the shadows, the reassuring shape of the chest of drawers calmed and reassured her. With a sigh, Carrie raised herself up on to the pillow. It was another nightmare she'd had, that was all it was. But when she glanced at the clock beside her bed, she could see that she had barely been asleep.

'Oh, dear,' she whispered. 'What's happening to me? Why am I seeing these awful things?'

Were they a premonition of some impending doom? A warning?

Carrie lay back, trying to calm her tangled nerves and chiding herself for being so ridiculous. But then, moments later, as Aunt Lorna's face swam uninvited into her head, her thoughts whirled even more, and for a few brief, draining moments, her aunt's presence

46

seemed to fill the entire room. Carrie caught her breath. Had she inherited Lorna's psychic gifts? Was her aunt trying to warn her of something? And if she was, of what?

She shivered and shrugged the feeling off. She was being far too oversensitive, overwhelmed by phantoms of the past. After all, hadn't Aunt Lorna always said that she didn't have the gift? When, at last, Carrie fell into a fitful slumber, she prayed Aunt Lorna was right!

CHAPTER FOUR

Heavy-eyed, Carrie awoke next morning and turned to face the open window. She hadn't slept well and, for long, lethargic moments, lay staring at the wafting, floral curtains. Vague, unfamiliar shadows had haunted her, leaving her restless and depressed. But now, as she welcomed the new day, its cheerful promise was a reassuring sight.

Carrie threw back the duvet and swung out of bed, determined to thrust her nightmares to the back of her mind. There were lots of things she must do today. The rest of her clothes needed to be put away, and her few items of furniture were due to arrive at ten. And, on top of that, it was also necessary to go through Aunt Lorna's effects and store away the things she didn't need, and pick out the ones that she did.

Throwing on a robe, Carrie made her way down to the kitchen and switched on the kettle, unlocking the conservatory door and inhaling deeply the sweet, morning air. Glancing up into the clear sky, she gave a little smile. It was going to be a beautiful day! She was feeling better already! The kettle boiled and she poured herself a mug of coffee, then took it, along with the morning's post, into the conservatory. A glance at the envelopes told her that there wasn't much of interest today. Putting them to one side and finishing her coffee, she went back upstairs.

Half an hour later, dressed, and wearing the minimum of make-up, Carrie went back down again, determined to make a start on her chores. She opted to sort out her own clothes first before going into Aunt Lorna's room to go through her things. That wasn't a chore she was relishing! The very thought of it was making her feel uncomfortable. To Carrie, it seemed an impertinence to disturb anything that had belonged to her very private and secretive aunt.

It needed to be done though, and with a resigned sigh, she started on the task of placing her underwear neatly away into the lavender-scented drawers of the old-fashioned dressing-table, and finding room in a closet to stack her shoes.

However, it wasn't very long before her plans were interrupted.

The sound of footsteps outside caused Carrie to glance up and look out of the window. A man was at the door and, as he pressed the bell causing her heart to lift in the hope it might be James, she hurried downstairs to answer it. But it wasn't James. With a small shock of surprise, she opened the door to find Steve Butler standing there.

'Hello, Steve!' Carrie greeted him brightly, hoping her disappointment didn't show too

49

much. 'This is a surprise! Do come in. What brings you round to Dell Cottage so early in the morning?'

'Hi, Carrie!'

At her invitation he stepped inside, giving her a rueful little smile.

'Any chance of a coffee?'

'Of course!'

'My car's on the blink. I was on my way to Trefwr to pick up a package from the station when it started to splutter.'

'Oh, dear!'

'I didn't want to risk being stuck on the mountain road so I've left it at the garage by the crossroads.'

He shrugged apologetically.

'They said it would be about an hour before they got it fixed so, as you are so near, I thought I'd come and dump myself on you. I hope you don't mind.'

'No problem.'

Carrie went to refill the kettle as Steve sat down heavily on a kitchen chair still complaining about his car. When, a minute or two later, she handed him a mug, he thanked her and added three heaped teaspoons of sugar from the bowl on the kitchen table.

'Are you settling back in OK?' he asked.

'Well, I'm beginning to.'

'Bit of a change coming back here after so long, isn't it?'

'I suppose so, but I'm looking forward to it.'

50

There was a pause. Steve had never been one for animated conversation, and as Carrie sat down opposite him and waited, she wondered vaguely what on earth to talk about. She and Steve had known each other since schooldays, but they had never been particularly close. He was a morose individual, always had been, and even as a boy he never had very much to say for himself, and had always been known as a loner. Most of those who knew him put it down to the terrible shock of his sister dying in such tragic circumstances all those years ago, and understood.

Regarding him now, Carrie couldn't help but feel sorry for the man. She had heard he had been married once, but she hadn't known his wife. And, from all accounts, the marriage hadn't lasted long either, with a divorce in less than two years.

Steve sipped his coffee, his eyes darting everywhere until they finally rested on the two open suitcases that were still in the hall.

'Still unpacking then?' he asked.

'Yes, I am, but there isn't much more to do.'

'If you need a lift with anything, I'll be glad to help. I always like to make myself useful if I can.'

'Well, thank you, Steve, but it's really not necessary,' and with a smile, Carrie added, 'My worldly goods are not that many.'

She glanced at her watch.

51

'As a matter of fact, the removal men are due any time now with the rest of my things, and they won't take me five minutes to sort out.'

Steve shrugged and mumbled something about he was there if she needed him, and when the conversation dried up again, Carrie ventured, 'How's your father, Steve? I haven't seen him for ages. Is he well?'

'So-so.'

Then he shook his head.

'Actually, no, he's not too good at all. But I suppose you probably know that he's not been in the best of health since Mam and little Megan . . . it's his heart, you know.'

Carrie nodded sympathetically.

'Yes. I'd heard he'd been ill,' Carrie replied.

He looked up quickly.

'You remember my sister, don't you?'

'Of course, I do. Who could forget that awful time?'

Steve nodded, his eyes bleak.

'My dad never got over it,' he told Carrie sadly, 'nor my mam. They both suffered badly. And when Mam died the death certificate said it was from pneumonia, but we all knew that the real cause was a broken heart.'

Carrie shook her head again as Steve went on.

'It seems to get worse as each year passes. It's the not knowing that's the worst, you know. And, come Thursday, it'll be exactly fifteen years since it happened, and on the same day, too.'

Gently, she asked, 'Did no-one ever find out why Megan was so far from home that day? Or how she got to Ty Mynydd all by herself?'

He shook his head again.

'No, but someone must have taken her. She'd never have roamed off like that all on her own.'

Carrie was inclined to agree. Megan would have been about three-years-old when they found her, and Ty Mynydd was a good six miles from Tyr Gwyn, much too far for a toddler to walk on her own.

Steve swallowed down the remainder of his coffee and then, somewhat disconcertingly, fixed his gaze on Carrie for several long moments.

'Did your Aunt Lorna ever say anything about what happened to Megan?' he asked.

With a start, Carrie returned his stare.

'Aunt Lorna? Why would she?'

He shrugged, his head lowering.

'It's just that after the accident, Mam came to see Lorna a lot. She said that Lorna knew things. You know what I mean, don't you?'

Carrie felt the colour creep into her face. She knew exactly what Steve meant! And when she made no answer, he went on.

'Your aunt seemed to comfort my mother, and from what Mam told us, it was almost as though Lorna had seen the whole thing. Mam

53

said that there were two of them up at Ty Mynydd that day and that—'

He broke off, rubbing his hand across his forehead.

'Anyway,' he went on wearily, 'when Mam died I spoke to Lorna myself, tried to find out what she and Mam had talked about, but she wouldn't tell me anything except to let Mam rest in peace, like my sister.'

He gave a deep, ragged sigh.

'Peace! There'll be no peace till we know the truth.'

With her heart going out to this troubled young man, Carrie said gently, 'Look, Steve, my aunt couldn't have known anything about Megan's accident. How could she? Perhaps all she gave your mother was a few words of comfort and, being in such a distressed state, your mam wanted to see more in them than there really was.'

He nodded.

'Yes, you're probably right. But all the same—'

But just then, and to Carrie's relief, the sight of a van arriving in the driveway prevented any more discussion. Her bits and pieces had arrived, and with the help of Steve Butler and the two removal men, it wasn't very long before her desk, lap-top, books and other personal odds and ends were dispersed round the cottage.

'I'd better ring the garage,' Steve said when

the removal men had left. 'My car must be ready by now. I've been here well over an hour.'

He reached into his pocket for his mobile phone and pressed a number, and with a couple of OKs he confirmed that the car was ready.

'Thanks for your help, Steve,' Carrie said as she saw him to the door. 'Will I see you at rehearsal tonight?'

'More than likely. I should be back from Trefwr in plenty of time.'

And with a brief wave, he was gone.

*   *   *

James looked around with an impatient frown. The place was looking more like a building site than the elegant sitting-room he was hoping for. Everywhere, there were pots of paint and rolls of wallpaper, but no sign of a workman. He glanced at his watch. Probably they were all off on one of their breaks again! He strolled into his study, which, for the moment at least, was still reasonably habitable and flicked on his computer and prepared to settle down to a few hours of routine work.

Just turned thirty, James conveyed a restless energy that turned many a female head, although he had never been aware of it. And now, as he scanned his work on the screen, his concentration lapsed and he found his mind

55

drifting to the girl at Dell Cottage, and to her aunt, Lorna Davies.

'Look after my girl, James,' Lorna had asked him. 'There's danger in the village and I worry that I won't be here to look after her myself.'

James had laughed, dismissing Lorna's impending fears, but the old lady had insisted. 'Promise me, James,' she had implored him. 'Give me your solemn promise that you will look after her when I'm not here!'

'Very well, I promise,' he had assured her. 'But you'll outlive all of us, have no fear of that.'

But, in spite of his amused assurance, Lorna's expression had still betrayed her concern.

With a deep sigh, James got up and walked over to pour himself a drink, and as he sipped the whisky he realised again how wrong his words had been. Two months later he had been on the other side of the world and Lorna was no more. He had come back to Tyr Gwyn, bought Danyderi, and was determined to keep his promise. He would certainly have no problem with his duty. He had only been in Carrie's company twice but he was already half in love.

His eyes narrowed. He couldn't say why but, lately, he had sensed that the danger Lorna had warned of was real enough. He could feel it. It was all around Tyr Gwyn, bubbling just below the surface. Trouble was, how could he recognise it? James finished his drink and went back to his computer. For the moment, all he could do was to keep his ear to the ground, and his eyes on Carrie. He glanced up again to stare indecisively at the telephone. Should he give her a ring?

*   *   *

With Steve Butler and the removal men long gone, Carrie made herself a bite to eat and then made her way upstairs to Lorna's room. Best to get this part over with so, opening the door, Carrie stepped in and glanced around at the familiar objects, from the large, old-fashioned bed to the chest of drawers which was now covered by a light film of dust. Since the funeral, this had been the only room that Carrie had not entered.

She moved forward, sitting on the edge of the bed and wondering where to start. As the room darkened with the threat of an impending storm, Carrie suddenly began to feel a little lost. Rising to her feet, and swallowing her guilt, she began her task, starting with the wardrobe. She peered inside at the rows of dresses that were placed in an orderly fashion on their hangers, unusual for Aunt Lorna, and as she lifted them out one by one, folding them and placing them in a plastic bag, it surprised her to realise how many dresses Aunt Lorna owned, and how many pairs of shoes, too, all placed neatly on the shelf above her head.

She emptied the drawers, putting everything in various bags. When she was almost finished, she sat back on the bed holding the few, precious memories of her aunt that she wanted to keep. She glanced down at the photograph in her hand. It was in a pretty, redwood frame, and was one she remembered very well. It had been taken on Carrie's tenth birthday, when Aunt Lorna had surprised her with a few days' holiday in Scotland. They had been in Edinburgh that day.

Carrie recalled the day with affection and her heart swelled. She looked down at the picture of herself, a laughing child, perched on a wall, and at the woman who had brought her up so well. Tears filled her eyes, and she outlined her aunt's smiling face with her fingertip.

'Dear Aunt Lorna,' she murmured, 'how will I ever repay you?'

As Carrie sat there, so quietly in thought, she could almost feel her aunt's presence, especially so when her nostrils became aware of the gentle fragrance of lavender that still clung to the lace-edged pillow. For many more moments, memories were all around until, rousing herself, she put the picture down. There was still one last cupboard to go through.

Moving across the room, she turned the catch of the corner cupboard and pulled open the door, surprised to find that there was nothing in there except a carved, wooden box. Puzzled, Carrie reached in and drew it out, even more surprised that a box so small could be so heavy. Intrigued, she carried it over to the bedside table and opened it. Inside lay an object covered by a square piece of linen and, becoming even more intrigued, she drew the linen away to expose five large segments of glass.

With a little gasp she stared down at the crystal that was lying there, realising at once that these were what Aunt Lorna had always regarded as her crystal ball. As Carrie reached in to pick out a piece, her hands began to tremble.

She held it up to the light, never really believing that such a thing existed, long since putting any mention of seeing it in her crystal ball down to Aunt Lorna's quirky imagination. For a long time, Carrie couldn't move and, from outside, she could hear the storm raging round the cottage, as though eerily on cue. And then, turning her head towards the window as though looking for inspiration and finding none, she turned to look again at the heavy chunks of glass.

In total disbelief, and with her hands shaking slightly, Carrie scooped up all the pieces and carried them over to the windowsill, to stand gazing down at them for a long, long time. What did she expect to see? They were nothing more than a few shards of glass! And as she stared, the only thing she could see in them was a shadowy reflection of the ivy as it trailed from the cottage wall outside.

After a while, Carrie put them back into the box and covered them up again with their square of linen.

'For goodness' sake, girl, what's the matter with you?' she scolded herself. 'What did you expect to see? The end of the world?'

And then, as she put the box back into the cupboard and locked it away again, she gave a sudden start as she heard the phone ringing. She hurried downstairs to answer it.

'Hi! It's me!' James's voice came down the line.

'Oh, hi!' Carrie answered, her voice sounding surprised.

There was a brief pause, then, 'Are you OK?'

'Yes, of course, I'm OK,' she answered. 'I'm fine.'

'Are you sure?'

'Yes. I'm fine,' Carrie assured him again. 'Why shouldn't I be?'

'You sound . . . funny.'

There was another brief pause, then, 'Are you going to the rehearsal?'

'I'm hoping to, yes,' Carrie replied, with a quickening of her heartbeat.

60

'Shall I pick you up?'

'There's no—'

Then Carrie paused. It would be nice to have a little company tonight. It had been a very strange day, and the discovery of the crystals had shaken her more than she realised, so after a moment, Carrie admitted, 'Yes, I think I'd like that.'

'Fine. Shall we say around seven?'

'Yes, seven will be fine. I'll be ready.'

CHAPTER FIVE

By seven o'clock the storm had passed over and Carrie, already showered and changed, heard a car pull up outside. A quick glance through the window told her it was James so, snatching up her bag and keys, she went out to meet him.

Although the rain had stopped, drops still lay heavy on the trees and they felt like cold, sharp needles as they fell on Carrie's head as she ran towards his car. As she reached it, James swung over and pushed open the passenger door.

'Hi!' he said cheerfully as she climbed in. 'You OK?'

'Yes, thanks.'

'Some storm, wasn't it?'

'Certainly was. Still, do the gardens good, as they say.'

'That's what they say.'

James made a turn and they set off for the school.

'Are you sure you're OK?' he asked again.

Carrie threw him a quick glance.

'Why do you keep asking if I'm OK?'

'Because you sounded a bit odd when I rang. Sort of tense. I got the feeling that maybe something was wrong.'

'Well, it's nice to know you're concerned

about me,' she responded with a wry smile, 'but there's nothing wrong, honestly. I'd just been going through Aunt Lorna's things, so I suppose I was a bit keyed up, that's all.'

'I see.'

He threw her a brief, sidelong glance, noticing, not for the first time, how tempting her lips were. He hoped that it wouldn't be too long before he could put them to the test, but as this was neither the time nor the place, he had to shelve his aspirations and concentrate on his driving. It was a good ten miles from Dell Cottage to the school.

'Not a very nice job,' he went on a few moments later, 'although I confess I've never had to do it myself. When my parents died my sister took care of all that side of things.'

What a typical male remark that was, Carrie thought, and at the same time, quite illogically, felt a small stir of surprise that he had a sister. It was the first time he'd mentioned his family, and she realised what a lot she had yet to learn about him. Somewhere in the back of her mind she was also wondering why she was the one he had elected to take to the rehearsal tonight, and not the delectable Adele Parry.

However, she made no comment about that and went on, 'It's a rotten job actually! I was dreading it, but it's done with now.'

'Good!'

Carrie turned to look out of the window. Mentioning Aunt Lorna had set her mind drifting back to the cottage, and to her discovery of the crystals.

'It's funny what old ladies keep locked away, isn't it?' she said.

James raised an enquiring eyebrow.

'Is it? I'm afraid I wouldn't know.'

'You must have heard of Lorna's famous crystal ball.'

'Who hasn't? But what about it?'

'I came across it in a cupboard. It gave me quite a shock.'

James seemed amused.

'Why? Did you see something in it?'

'Of course not!' she replied hastily. 'It just surprised me, that's all.'

'I suppose it would.'

'And it's not really a ball at all, you know.'

'Oh? What is it then?'

'A few fragments of glass wrapped up in a cloth. Quite disappointing really.'

'I suppose it would be.'

She threw him another sidelong glance, sensing that he wasn't particularly impressed by what she was telling him.

'I never really believed in it, either, you know, or that it even existed, but I know a lot of people did and in its powers,' she said defensively.

'Probably because they needed to.'

'What do you mean?'

'Sometimes, believing in an outside influence, something beyond logic, can help

64

people cope better with whatever misfortune life happens to chuck at them.'

'You mean people like Mrs Butler, little Megan's mother?'

'Why her particularly?' he asked quietly.

Carrie gave a deep sigh.

'Because Steve dropped in on me earlier today and we got to talking along those lines.'

James frowned, his expression becoming more sombre.

'What did he want?'

'He invited himself for coffee while his car, which had broken down, was being fixed.'

Carrie then proceeded to tell him about the conversation that had passed between herself and Steve Butler earlier that day, and of the way he was still so badly affected by the loss of his little sister.

'That was a bad business,' James murmured when she had finished. 'It must have upset the whole village at the time.'

'It did. I remember it well,' Carrie said sadly.

She closed her eyes briefly, her thoughts suddenly focusing on the day Megan Butler went missing, and she was seeing again in her mind's eye how the men of the village set off on their vain search for her. She still felt the numbness when she'd seen the two policemen knocking on the Butlers' front door, one of them with his hand tightly clenched around the bedraggled little doll. Carrie shivered, vaguely conscious of James's voice stirring her back to the present.

'It was certainly odd that a young kid could wander off so far on her own,' she heard him say. 'I still hear rumours from time to time, you know, the odd word.'

'What kind of odd word?'

'Well, you know, kidnapping, for instance. Abduction.'

'Abduction?'

'Yes, it's come up from time to time. In fact, I remember coming over to visit Lorna one time and first hearing that particular word mentioned.'

He paused fractionally as he slowed down for a set of traffic lights.

'And if my memory serves me right she used that same word only a few weeks before she died.'

'To you?'

'Yes, in a way. I'd popped round to see her, as I recall, and just as I turned into the drive, the side door opened and your aunt and Mrs Butler came out. They didn't see me at first, but I could tell that Mrs Butler was in a pretty distressed state. Lorna had her arms around her and it was obvious she was trying to console the poor woman, although it didn't seem to be having much effect. Then they saw me and Mrs Butler hurried away.'

'And did my aunt say why Mrs Butler was so upset?'

James shook his head.

'Not exactly, but as we went into the cottage I heard her say something about how hard it was for Mrs Butler to cope and how she, Lorna, couldn't help. She said Megan's mother was convinced that her daughter would still be alive today if someone hadn't persuaded her to go with them up to Ty Mynydd, someone she must have known and trusted.'

Carrie stared at him, suddenly feeling very cold.

'How awful. How dreadful it must have been to think that someone had taken your child.'

He nodded morosely.

'Yes, it must.'

She looked at him, seeing compassion in his eyes, but also something else. Was it speculation? Reserve? Carrie couldn't tell.

'And you do believe it?' she asked.

'About someone taking Megan? I really don't know. Seems a bit strong to me. I mean, we're talking about kidnap, aren't we? For what reason would anyone want to do that? It couldn't have been for the money, could it? The Butlers aren't exactly rolling in it, are they?'

'Far from it.'

'Still,' James went on, 'it doesn't necessarily have to be for financial gain. There could have been other reasons, I suppose.'

'Such as?'

He gave Carrie a quick glance, conscious of the impact his words were having on her.

'Look,' he continued, 'I'm only making conjectures. It was probably an accident, tragic, true, but an accident just the same. The child wandered too far away from home and got lost. Sadly, it happens all the time. You can read about such things almost every day.'

Carrie shivered again, and a cold little twist lurched in her stomach as she turned quickly to James.

'You said other reasons.'

He gave a resigned sigh.

'Look, let's drop it, shall we?'

'No! Tell me, James. In Megan Butler's case, if she was lured away by someone, what other reason could there be if it wasn't for money?'

James shook his head, wishing he'd never mentioned his suspicions, suspicions which were now clearly giving Carrie such alarm.

'Well, there are things such as jealousy, revenge.'

'Jealousy? But who could be jealous of a three-year-old? And how on earth could such a little girl cause anyone to seek revenge?'

'Look, Carrie . . .'

'And even if any of it was true, who would do such a thing?'

'Look,' James repeated, 'forget what I've said. I don't know what happened any more than you do.'

'Perhaps not, but you do have your suspicions, don't you? And you must have your reasons to say such things, or even to think such things.'

'I have no reason to think anything. But if something terrible did happen to that little girl, then—'

James broke off, realising he was making things worse.

'Then what?'

He sighed. Clearly, Carrie was not about to let things drop now so, very reluctantly, he might as well tell her the rest of his misgivings.

'I was just thinking that, well, whoever might have been involved, then they are probably still around.'

Carrie frowned. The last thing she wanted to do was to believe what James was saying, but in her heart of hearts she knew it was quite possible. Although she had never realised it before, it dawned on her now that there had always been something about Megan Butler's disappearance that had puzzled and confounded her. No reason had ever been found for the distance which separated Megan from her home. How had she got there? Had she really been alone? Or had someone deliberately taken her up to Ty Mynydd that day?

There was something else that nagged at her, too, and Carrie's heart missed a beat as she realised what it was. No-one had ever proved that the child had left her house alive! And why, if a child had wandered off in play, would she leave her favourite doll behind? After all, the whole village knew that Megan and her doll had been inseparable!

An awkward silence followed, and Carrie felt her heart still bumping against her ribs. James glanced at her.

'What are you thinking, Carrie?'

She raised her eyes to his, causing his heart to thud, and he wondered, momentarily, if she could tell from his expression how much he was beginning to care for her.

'What you say,' she said at last, 'it's very difficult. I shall have to think about it for a while.'

'Carrie,' he responded quietly, his reflexes masking his concern, 'I've told you, it's only my conjecture. The last thing in the world I would want is for you to be worried about something that probably didn't happen.'

'But you think it might have, don't you?'

'I only say it's possible.'

'And I'm inclined to agree.'

'You are?'

'Yes, I am. Please tell me exactly what you feel about it. Maybe, between us, we can make some sense of it.'

There was another pause, very slight, then James, taking a deep breath, said, 'Well, OK, if you really want my opinion.'

'I do.'

'There isn't really much to say and, even if there was, I'm damned if we can do anything about it now. It's so long ago.'

'I know, but tell me, James. Tell me what else you're thinking.'

'Well, the way I see it, if someone caused little Megan's death, be it accidentally or deliberately, I wouldn't be at all surprised to find that that someone was someone Megan knew, and trusted. And I'd bet anything you like that someone is still around Tyr Gwyn.'

Sombrely, Carrie nodded.

'I would agreed with that. Isn't it true that in most mysteries, it's usually the one thing that's under everyone's nose that's the hardest to see?'

'Very true. And there's something else.'

'What?'

'Don't you think it's odd that no-one's heard from Josie?'

'Josie?'

She hadn't expected that and, stunned, Carrie looked at James. He was very still, but she saw how his knuckles gleamed white as they rested on the wheel, and she noticed, too, the strained set to his mouth.

'What on earth has Josie got to do with it?'

'I'm not sure, but I have a very strong feeling that she has.'

'What's caused such a feeling? Are you saying you think there might be a connection?'

James shrugged.

'I don't know,' he answered slowly. 'As I say, it's only a feeling I have. Call it instinct if you like.'

For a long moment Carrie stared at James. Then, drawing a deep breath in an effort to rationalise her confusion, she turned away to look out of the window again, and at the approaching lights of the village ahead. Strangely, she was feeling a sense of disappointment. She had expected more from him than that.

'For a moment there I thought you had something more tangible on which to base your suspicions. But is that all you have to go on? Your instinct?'

'For the moment, yes.'

'Well,' she responded, 'I would rather rely on a little more than that, James. Don't forget, I was raised by a psychic and, love her as I did, she often caused me lots of problems. I have no wish to get involved with another!'

She heard James's deep sigh.

'Sorry,' he answered eventually. 'I didn't mean it to sound like that. What I meant was—'

'Never mind!' Carrie interrupted.

And so, for a short time they drove on in silence. James accepted Carrie's rebuke and decided against any elaboration on what he actually did mean. However, as he drove the car into the school's parking area he turned to her.

'May I say just one more thing before we join the others for rehearsal?'

'What's that?'

He found her hand and squeezed it tightly.

'I rather like the thought of the two of us being involved as you so nicely put it,' he said quickly.

'Oh!' Carrie was momentarily flustered. 'I—I—'

He gave her hand another brief squeeze as she turned to face him. She sensed he had moved nearer, but he hadn't, but yet her skin prickled.

'Tell you what,' he went on, 'if there is anything to find out about young Megan's disappearance, promise me you won't do anything on your own.'

He looked at her silently for a moment.

'If you hear anything, anything at all, promise me you'll tell me first and we'll find out about it together.'

Carrie gave a light, nervous laugh.

'But what is there to—'

'Promise me!'

She felt herself flush at his urgent manner.

'Very well!' she retorted. 'I promise!'

'Good!'

He took his hand away. The touch had been very disturbing.

CHAPTER SIX

Natalie's agitated voice greeted them as they pushed open the door of the rehearsal hall, and as she rose to meet them a look of relief was written all over her flushed face.

'James! Carrie! Thank goodness! At least you've managed to turn up! Hardly anyone's shown face tonight,' she went on disdainfully, 'and it can only be because of the storm. I'd no idea my cast was such a bunch of softies, letting a drop of rain keep them from their practice.'

Carrie glanced around with a faintly startled air, thinking that perhaps Natalie was exaggerating somewhat. True, the numbers seemed slightly down on the last rehearsal but not by that many. As far as she could tell, most of the chorus was accounted for. On stage, some were going through their routine for a dance, and a separate group was at the far end of the room practising a number. The only absent faces seemed to be those of Adele Parry, Mark Jones, Eddie Powell and Steve Butler.

'I was hoping to do the wedding scene tonight,' Natalie was saying as Carrie and James, acknowledging Jean's wave of hello, moved farther into the room. 'I never thought for a moment that Adele wouldn't turn up,

74

especially now it's certain that she'll play the lead. But how can Ian do the scene without her? It's one of the most touching in the whole show. And it has to be just right!'

'Hey! Can someone give me a lift with this?'

The yell came from one of the props boys as he struggled with a bulky piece of scenery.

'Hold on!' James called back. 'I'll give you a hand!'

As two other willing volunteers dashed to help as well, James excused himself and went off towards the stage. Meanwhile, Natalie, still grumbling, returned to her coaching of the chorus line. Suddenly finding herself alone, Carrie cast a glance around and wondered how she, too, could make herself useful. She finally opted for tidying up a pile of discarded scores scattered along a nearby table, putting them into some kind of order.

Presently, she was aware that the table she was using had another occupant. A young, dark-haired woman with a rather bored air about her had perched herself against the opposite corner, and after a moment's hesitation, began to speak.

'You're Carrie Davies, aren't you?'

When Carrie acknowledged that she was, the girl went on.

'Steve's told me about you. You live in that lovely cottage over by the bridge, don't you? I'm Pam Levens.'

'Hi!' Carrie said and accepted the girl's firm

handshake.

'I don't suppose you know what's happened to him, do you?' the girl asked.

'Who? Steve?' and when the girl nodded, Carrie shook her head. 'I'm afraid not.'

'He said he'd definitely be here tonight,' Pam went on, her accent sounding more English than local. 'He promised to bring his CD of the show for me to listen to. I'm playing Graziella, you know.'

'Oh, really?' Carrie responded. 'I didn't know that was a singing part.'

'It isn't. I'm a dancer, but I wanted to listen to the music anyway.'

'I saw Steve last night,' another voice came.

Turning to look in its direction, Carrie recognised Olwen Phillips, a tall, slender girl with pretty auburn hair and good features, and whom Carrie knew had quite a weakness for the more gullible members of the male population of Tyr Gwyn.

'He was in the White Hart with Mark,' she told them, 'but they didn't stay long. Left about nine.'

'Did he say anything about not coming tonight?' Pam Levens asked.

Olwen shook her head.

'No, not a word. But then, neither he nor Mark spoke to us anyway. Come to think of it, they didn't let on to anyone all evening, just stood at the bar with their heads together as though they had some secret.'

'What were they up to, do you think?' Pam asked.

'Who knows? They probably weren't up to anything really. They just seemed to be acting a bit mysteriously. Mind you, that's nothing unusual with the men around here, especially when they're talking about football or rugger. Although I have to say, they did seem to be deeper into conversation than they usually are. Anyway, they left without a word, or even a glance at anyone else.'

She looked at Carrie and then at Pam Levens, clearly enjoying their attention.

'And between you and me,' she went on with a little smirk, 'I think Adele was quite miffed about it. I could tell that by the way she glowered at them when they passed our table. She's not having much luck with her men lately. She really went all out to hook James Alexander but he wasn't having any. I can't make out yet whether she's turned her attention to Mark or Steve now.'

Overhearing the tail-end of the conversation, Natalie stepped forward.

'So you were with Adele last night?'

Olwen nodded.

'Yes, and with a couple of other friends as well.'

'Did Adele give any hint that she might miss tonight's rehearsal?' Natalie asked, a little tersely. 'Did she seem ill, or anything?'

Olwen's dark head shook again.

'No, she seemed OK. As far as I'm concerned she was going to be here, and we were going to go back to her flat afterwards for a glass of wine.'

Olwen reached into her bag for her mobile phone.

'No problem though. I can give her a ring if you like, to find out what's happened.'

'No, never mind.'

Natalie, somewhat disgruntled, muttered something about unreliability and as she turned to rejoin the others, Pam and Olwen also moved away, leaving Carrie to finish sorting out the scores. Gradually the rehearsal began to break up, and James made his way back to Carrie's side.

'How does a glass of wine sound to you?' he murmured. 'This acting lark's given me quite a thirst.'

She looked up at him, smiling.

'Fancy the White Hart?'

'Good choice! But why the White Hart particularly?'

'No particular reason. It's just that from what I hear it seems to be where the action might be.'

But as it turned out there was no action at the White Hart that evening. It appeared that everyone had decided either to make their way home or to visit some other local. So, after one drink, they agreed to call it a day and James drove her home.

Fumbling with her key in the doorway, James's hand shot out and took it from her.

'Allow me.'

He unlocked the door and let Carrie through.

'Like some coffee?' she asked him, tossing her bag on to a nearby chair.

'Won't say no. Black, please, and lots of sugar. I mustn't stay long, though. I've an early start tomorrow. I'll just hang on for five minutes to make sure you're OK.'

Carrie threw him a grin as she switched on the kitchen light.

'Taking care of me again?'

'Of course!'

'Better make yourself at home then.'

She shrugged off her jacket and hung it on its hook in the closet, then flicked on the percolator. She also switched on the subdued lighting in the conservatory.

'And where are you off to that calls for an early start?' she asked.

'Aberdeen. Should be back by mid-afternoon, though.'

'What's taking you all the way up to Scotland?'

'I'm delivering a private plane for some bigwig industrialist.'

Carrie laughed.

'And how will you get back? Will you have to thumb a lift?'

James laughed, too.

'Not quite. They're laying on a helicopter for me.'

For the next few minutes James watched Carrie as she spooned brown sugar into two yellow ceramic mugs, thoroughly enjoying watching her. Then, as she handed him his coffee, she suggested they drink it in the comfort of the conservatory. Carrie curled herself into the striped wicker sofa and let her shoes fall to the floor, while James settled into the opposite chair.

For the next few moments neither spoke, both trying to relax in the pleasant, easy atmosphere and, each unknown to the other, thinking what a very nice feeling it was to be sharing the evening together. But pleasant as it was, Carrie's mind still refused to relax entirely, and her thoughts soon began to circle yet again to the situation of Josie's long absence, and of the tragedy of Megan. She looked at James, her expression serious.

'Actually, James,' she began quietly, 'there is something I'd like to ask you now that we're alone.'

'OK,' he answered, 'ask away.'

'Do you remember when we were talking earlier about kidnapping and those other awful things?' Carrie queried, her voice low.

'I remember. What about it?'

'Well, I know you said it was more a gut instinct.'

She paused, her face wary.

'Yes, go on,' he encouraged.

'Well, what I'm trying to say is, what made you think that Josie might be connected with any of it?'

James sighed and placed his mug on the table between them.

'I don't know that there's any connection. It's because of something that happened once, quite a while ago now.'

'Oh? What was that?'

He screwed up his eyes in concentration.

'Let's see, it would be about a month before you came back to the cottage. I'd moved into Danyderi and by then had got to know everyone in the village pretty well. I'd got to know Josie quite well, and Steve Butler. From the way they acted whenever they were together, I soon began to suspect that they liked each other well enough to believe that a relationship might blossom between them.'

'Josie and Steve?' Carrie said, intrigued.

'Yes. The thing was, you see, she was doing some work for me at the time, some filing work I needed putting into some kind of order, and when she was at the house she'd let the odd thing slip. I soon was able to tell that she was beginning to like Steve quite a lot but he was still married then, of course, although his divorce was going through. Anyway, he was in a pretty bad way emotionally and I think Josie felt sorry for him to start with. She used to tell me how she'd try to jolly him out of his

81

depression, and how she would support him all the way, no matter how many problems he had.'

'Yes,' Carrie commented. 'Josie would do that. She was always very kind-hearted.'

'Steve, naturally, was grateful to her,' James continued, 'and appreciative. But, gradually, gratitude turned into something else, and the friendship, on both sides, became a lot more serious.'

Carrie drew a deep breath. She was hearing now, in his calm, deep words, something she could identify with.

'But there's nothing wrong with falling in love with someone, is there?'

'Nothing at all! In fact, I'm all for it,' he replied lightly.

'Then why should Josie disappear? Did they have a quarrel? Did something go wrong?'

'I don't know,' James replied. 'But don't you start reading things into it and become afraid. Josie's going away is probably nothing to do with anything. Trouble is, there's more. I gave her a lift home one day and she seemed very excited about something. She asked me if I would drop her off at Steve's place as she had something to tell him. She wouldn't tell me what it was, but she did tell me one thing, and it's that one thing that's worrying me now.'

'What is it, James?'

'Well, as I drove her into the village she told me that she'd discovered something about what had happened at Ty Mynydd on the day that Megan died, and that Steve ought to know about it.'

'But what had she discovered? How did she discover it? What was it?'

'I couldn't get any more out of her. She wouldn't tell me. She said she wanted Steve to hear it before she told anyone else so I had to let it drop. But then, when I pulled up at the end of Butler's street and she got out, she saw something, and whatever that something was, it scared her. Instead of going up to Steve's house as I'd expected, she suddenly turned and ran off in the opposite direction, and her face was like a sheet.'

'What did she see, do you think?'

'I don't know. When she ran off I called her back, but she either didn't hear me, or deliberately chose not to. Anyway, within minutes she was gone! Disappeared! And I remember getting out of the car and looking everywhere but I couldn't see anything or anyone.'

'Whatever could it have been?'

'I don't know,' he repeated, his face grim. 'But there was definitely something. I went up to Steve's house to tell him about it, but he wasn't in. The place was deserted. I didn't know what else to do, so, after a while, I drove home intending to ring him later.'

'And did you?'

'Yes, but he'd no idea what it was that Josie

had wanted to tell him, nor did he ever find out. You see, it was the very next day that Josie went away, and no-one's heard from her since.'

'Shouldn't we tell the police all of this?'

'I already have, but there's really nothing for them to go on, no suspicious circumstances.'

'I don't like it, James,' Carrie murmured. 'I don't like it at all.'

'Nor do I, and now, perhaps, you'll understand why I feel that there's something odd going on around here, and why I don't want you to do anything without letting me know.'

'I agree. And I won't. I promise.'

'Look, Carrie, I really can't stay longer than a couple more minutes.'

It took rather longer than a couple of minutes, however, for Carrie and James to wish each other good-night. They sat together in the conservatory, chatting for almost another hour until, finally, he rose to take his leave.

'May I see you tomorrow?' he asked as they stood close together.

'If you like.'

'Shall we go for a bite to eat? We could try that new Chinese place in Trefwr if you like. Everyone says it's worth a visit.'

'Yes, I'd like that. I'll look forward to it.'

He lowered his head and his lips brushed her cheek, and even that simple movement set her heart thudding and when, moments later, his mouth touched hers, they were soon holding each other in a deep, lingering kiss. With a long sigh James finally tore himself away.

'Must go now. See you tomorrow,' he murmured.

After a final, warm embrace he climbed into his car and started the engine. As she watched him drive away, Carrie's eyes were bright. In spite of their worrying conversation regarding Josie, a kind of peace was filling her and she could hardly wait until she saw him again tomorrow. She stood looking up at the stars for several more minutes before making her way back into the cottage to rinse out the two mugs that were still on the conservatory table.

Then, in the hallway, something caught her eye and she suddenly noticed the flashing light on her answering machine. Clearly, someone had been trying to contact her while she had been out at the rehearsal. It turned out to be a message from Steve Butler. And, standing there listening to it, her heart suddenly began to race.

'Hi, Carrie, it's Steve,' he said. 'I hope you haven't left for rehearsal yet and that you're still about somewhere. It's just that I won't be able to make it tonight and I can't get hold of Nat to let her know. Her mobile's switched off. Anyway, something's come up. I've had a message from Josie. Yes, Josie! She's OK! She wants to see me so I've arranged to meet her in Cardiff. She has something to tell me about our little Megan. Sorry I can't tell you more right now. I'll ring you when I get back.'

There was a click as the message ended and, trembling slightly, Carrie stared down at the machine. She rewound it and played it back three more times. Then, picking up the phone again, Carrie pressed out the digits of James's number. He answered after only one ring but his tone, when he spoke, sounded strangely flat and toneless.

'Carrie,' he said. 'I was just about to ring you. You've heard then?'

'Heard what, James?'

'About the accident! It's Steve Butler. He's been in an accident.'

It was as though Carrie's breath had been sucked out of her body.

'He rang me, James, when we were at rehearsal. There's a message on my machine. I was ringing to tell you.'

She caught her breath.

'James, is Steve hurt?'

There was a short pause, then James, in that same flat monotone, said, 'I'm afraid he's dead, Carrie. He died before they could get him to the hospital.'

She stood transfixed. Surely there had been some mistake. It just couldn't be true!

'Carrie!'

James's voice came down the line, rousing her from her state of shock.

'Carrie!' he called again. 'Can you hear me?'

She gave herself a mental shake.

'Yes, yes, James, I can hear you.'

'Look! I'm coming over,' he said, his voice sounding very anxious.

'No, there's no need, honestly. I'm all right.'

'Then will you do something for me?'

'If I can.'

'Will you go round to Jean's tomorrow and stay with her until I get back from Aberdeen?'

'But why?'

'Please! Will you, Carrie? For my sake?'

She let out a resigned sigh.

'Very well, James. If it will make you feel better I'll spend the day with Jean. I only hope I won't be in her way.'

'I'm sure you won't. Well, good-night, love, and sweet dreams. See you tomorrow.'

After the click of her phone ended their talk, James stood motionless for a long time, his thoughts racing. Although he hadn't said as much to Carrie, he was convinced that what had happened to Steve Butler tonight was more than an accident and it was causing him some anxiety. If anything should happen to Carrie!

Snatching up his jacket, he strode out of the house, climbed into his car and headed directly towards Dell Cottage. With his mind shying away from the thought of danger, James turned up his collar and settled down to spend the night in his car. After all, hadn't he promised to be her guardian angel?

At first light, James roused himself from an uncomfortable night, took a look at the peaceful cottage and started up the engine. With a final glance up at Carrie's window, he turned and headed towards Cardiff airport.

CHAPTER SEVEN

After a fitful night of tossing and turning, Carrie was relieved to see the day finally break across the night sky. She swung out of bed, slipping on her robe and, as she made her way downstairs, she wondered if James was already on his way to Aberdeen. With a wry smile as she made her morning coffee, she acknowledged that his wishes for her to have sweet dreams had certainly not been granted!

Outside the kitchen window the early-morning sun was already showing a watery face, and as Carrie switched on the kettle, she found her thoughts turning once again to the Butler family, and to their tragedy over Steve. Carrie sighed, turning quickly to pick up the phone. The coffee had warmed her, but all thoughts of food were out of the question and, true to her promise to James, she rang Jean Owen's number. When Jean's voice came down the line, sounding shocked and dismayed, Carrie quickly arranged to go over to spend the day with them. Jean's relief was palpable.

'Come as soon as you can, Carrie,' she said. 'This has knocked the stuffing out of all of us. It will be good to have someone here to talk to.'

'I'll be with you as soon as I can.'

Carrie rang off. Like Jean, she was feeling the need to talk to someone, too, and half an hour later she was driving through the narrow, winding lanes which would lead her to their large, comfy house. As she drove, a small frown began to show faintly along her forehead. Something in James's tone had disturbed her last night. It wasn't so much what he had said, but more in the way of how he had said it. He had sounded anxious, and seemed overly-insistent that she did exactly as he asked. She had been too tired and too much in shock about Steve to pursue the question with him then, but did he feel that she was in some danger, too? But if so, why?

Carrie gave a deep sigh. Too many strange things seemed to be happening in the village, too many strange coincidences. Carrie began to think seriously, for the first time since her return to Dell Cottage, whether her decision to come back here had been such a wise one after all. And in the next few moments, as her mind leaped ahead, she also found herself wondering if she was in some danger would it perhaps be better if she were to get clean away right now?

Later on, perhaps, when she had time to think about it rationally, she would probably be angry with herself for feeling like she was at that moment. After all, it was through no-one's fault but her own that she had got herself embroiled in something she could barely understand. She ought to be angry now, but there was no time for that. Carrie was too preoccupied with Tyr Gwyn's immediate problem to indulge in righteous indignation. The fact that there might be a murderer about was enough for anyone to think about right now!

The road sloped downwards towards the River Dulas, and beyond that, through the hazy mist, she could see the range of mountains that zigzagged like a spiral staircase towards Ty Mynydd's peak. Then, some way ahead and around the next turn, Carrie saw the large, white-washed house that was her destination, the home of the Owen family. She turned the car into the drive and, almost at once, Jean's husband, David, came out to greet her. He was a big, stoutish man in shirt sleeves, and with a rich, deep voice that had long been an asset to the local choir.

'Carrie!' he welcomed, opening the driver's door. 'Jean tells me you're to spend the day with us. Come in! I believe the kettle's already on the boil.'

Carrie climbed out of her car and shook his broad hand.

'I hope you don't mind, David. I wouldn't want to be in the way.'

'You're never in the way,' he assured her, and adding somewhat conspiratorially as they took the few strides up to the cottage door, 'As a matter of fact, I'm glad you're here. This

91

business about Steve has knocked us all for six. We still can't believe it. Jean's in a bit of a state.'

Carrie threw him a quick, anxious glance.

'Has anyone found out what happened yet, David? What it was that caused the accident?'

He shook his head.

'Not really, but it was the sole topic in the post office this morning. Someone said they had heard that his brakes had failed but if that was the case no-one knows for sure what caused it.'

He sighed and pushed open the door for her to enter the house.

'It's tragic all the same. That family has had nothing but bad luck.'

Inwardly agreeing with him Carrie found Jean waiting for her in the kitchen. She had been crying and her face was strained and pale, and as she moved to greet Carrie with her customary hug, it was patently clear that she was still very close to tears.

'Isn't it terrible news, Carrie?' she murmured, pouring out the cups of tea with a shaky hand. 'Poor Steve. I still can't believe it.'

Carrie shook her head.

'No, I don't think any of us can.'

She unbuttoned her jacket and sat down at the table as Jean passed her a cup. Jean and David Owen's kitchen was a cosy place, and their three children were playing together on the rug with their mongrel dog, Scruff.

'Right! We'll be off then!' David told them, shrugging on a fleecy jacket and herding his children together. 'Say goodbye to Mummy and Auntie Carrie. Mustn't be late for school.'

Farewell hugs were duly exchanged and when David and the children had left for the school run, Jean pulled up a chair and joined Carrie at the table. Sitting together, they quietly sipped their tea, neither one feeling particularly talkative after last night's shocking news.

After a while, Carrie glanced at Jean. She was sitting, rigid and stiff, on the wooden kitchen chair and her grey, normally placid eyes seemed fixed on some imaginary image across the room.

'He rang me last night,' Carrie told Jean quietly when her cup was finally emptied.

Jean turned to Carrie sharply.

'Who rang you? Steve?'

'Yes. He left a message on my answering machine.'

'What did he say?'

'He wanted me to let Natalie know that he wasn't going to make it to the rehearsal because something had come up.'

'What was it? Did he say?'

'Yes, he did. He said he had had a message, a phone call, from Josie.'

'Josie!'

Jean's wide eyes began to look a little more frightened now.

'Did he say where she was? Is she all right?'

'Yes, she's OK. She's in Cardiff, I think. At least, that's where he was going to meet her.'

'Cardiff?'

Again Carrie nodded.

'He said she wanted to see him, to tell him something about Megan.'

'Megan?'

'Yes. He'd arranged to meet her and he said he would ring me when he got back, except . . .'

Carrie broke off, feeling the numbness of shock again.

'Except,' she went on quietly, 'as we now know, Steve never got to Cardiff.'

'No, he didn't. I don't like it, Carrie. Something terrible is going on around here, I'm sure of it. And what's more, I have this terrible feeling that what happened to Steve was no accident.'

'What makes you think that?' Carrie asked her friend.

'A feeling, a terrible feeling. It's something he said the other day when he came over here to see David about something to do with the choir committee. It was about four o'clock and—'

Jean broke off, her normal quiet control completely gone and she covered her face with her hands. Carrie reached across to pat her arm.

'Jean,' she soothed, 'try to calm yourself. Why don't you take a deep breath and tell me what it was Steve said that's upsetting you so much?'

'He started talking about Megan again. We know he never got over the accident, and he started saying something about he'd always known there was more to it than ever came out. And what was more, he said he would soon be able to prove it. I wonder what he meant by that, Carrie.'

Carrie frowned and shook her head.

'I don't know.'

'Besides,' Jean went on, 'I should have noticed.'

'Noticed what?'

'His attitude, his manner. He's been different lately, sort of into himself, if you know what I mean.'

'But Steve's never been a very out-going type, has he?'

'Oh, I know what you're saying, Carrie, but lately he's—'

Jean hesitated and broke off, suddenly uncomfortable, as though she felt she had already said too much, and although Carrie pressed her, Jean would say no more. For a long moment the two women sat in silence, both lost in their thoughts. Jean was becoming calmer now, more in control, and Carrie was relieved to see it.

Presently, Jean broke the silence and asked Carrie unexpectedly, 'Did you know that Steve and Josie had been seeing each other before she went away?'

'Yes, I'd heard they'd become good friends.'

'Quite a lot happened in Tyr Gwyn while you were up North.'

'Then why don't you fill me in? Bring me up to date. Who knows, perhaps between us we might find out what's been going on, if something has, or whether these accidents are no more than a series of very unfortunate incidents.'

Jean smiled a little nervously.

'And we might discover something that's best left alone.'

'Was anyone jealous of their relationship?' Carrie asked, mindful of James telling her of the day that Josie took flight when he'd given her a lift. 'Did someone else have their eye on her?'

Jean shook her head.

'Not that I know of. I can't imagine who, anyway.'

'Tell me what you can remember, even if it didn't seem important at the time. You never know, perhaps the answer is right under our noses.'

'I really can't think of anything.'

'Try, Jean, it could be important.'

'Well, I do remember we were all surprised when they began to spend so much time together. After all, Steve's divorce hadn't then come through and this village, as you know, has always shied clear of what it considers to be bad form. There were a few who disapproved.'

'Such as?'

'I can't really remember, although, come to think of it, Mark Jones suddenly springs to mind.'

'Mark Jones?'

'Yes. I remember one night when we had all met up in the White Hart after one of the rehearsals for the last show, and I remember it quite clearly because it was so out of character for Mark. I've never seen him lose his temper with anyone, have you?'

Carrie shook her head in agreement, then Jean went on.

'Yet, that night, he did lose it. We all heard him rowing with Steve.'

'What about? What was he saying?'

'It was something about Josie. I can't remember what exactly, but I do recall him saying that Steve was an idiot to get involved with her. Oh, wait a minute, I remember now! He said she had always been a born liar.'

Carrie's expression was incredulous.

'A born liar? Josie?'

'I'm sure that's what he said. It isn't something one would forget, is it?'

'But why should he say such a thing? I, for one, have never known Josie to be a liar. Quite the opposite, in fact.'

'Exactly! Honestly, Carrie, I don't know why he should say a thing like that, but we all heard him. Naturally, Steve, was furious. He rounded on Mark and they had a real set-to. The bad feeling between them went on for weeks, and it was a long time before the two of them spoke with any civility to each other after that. It gradually passed over, of course, and most of us forgot all about it. When Steve's divorce came through, and he and Josie started to get quite serious about each other, well, we all wished them well, all except Mark, that is. I noticed that he didn't exactly fall over himself to encourage them.'

'And Josie and Steve started going together seriously?'

'Very seriously. They were inseparable. They were even beginning to hint at an engagement.'

'So what was it, I wonder,' Carrie mused, almost to herself, 'that sent Josie away.'

For the moment, her question remained unanswered as the sound of another car turning into the drive caused both girls to glance towards the window. It was Natalie, and within minutes, she had joined them in the kitchen, her expression as shocked and stunned as Jean's.

'I'm calling off the show,' she told them briskly. 'It just wouldn't be right. All this terrible business about Steve has taken all the spark out of everyone.'

'I suppose it's the only decent thing to do,' Jean responded. 'I know that I, for one, am in no mood for singing and dancing.'

Natalie flopped down into the nearest chair.

'Nor am I, nor anybody, come to that. My mobile's been going mad all morning and Ian, Adele and Mark have already made it plain they would rather opt out.'

'Perhaps,' Carrie said with the ghost of a smile, 'later on, when a suitable time has passed, we could do it as a sort of dedication to Steve.'

Natalie looked at her in some relief.

'Yes, we could do that. That would be a nice thing to do for him. Perhaps—'

She broke off as the phone rang and Jean got up to answer it. It was James, asking to speak to Carrie.

'Hi!' his deep, pleasant voice came down the line. 'Everything all right?'

'Yes,' Carrie answered, relieved to hear him. 'Are you still in Aberdeen?'

'No, I'm back at Cardiff. Carrie, I have a couple of things to do here before I can meet you. May I come up to Dell Cottage later, about seven?'

'Of course.'

'Right. See you then.'

And he rang off.

CHAPTER EIGHT

James Alexander made his way across the carpark at Cardiff Airport. On the flight back from Aberdeen, after deciding to return on the shuttle rather than use the helicopter, he had been doing some serious thinking. Something intangible had been nagging at him for ages, and Steve Butler's fatal accident was all part of it.

He was convinced that everything was tied up with little Megan Butler and Josie Barnes, and the latter's abrupt departure from Tyr Gwyn. On the flight back to Wales, he'd been racking his brains to see if there was anything else he could remember about the day he had given Josie that final lift. He remembered vividly her sudden, startled look as she'd stepped out of his car. On the drive into town, she had been talking about her paintings and about a particular one which seemed to be causing her some anxiety. It was clear she was looking forward to talking it over with Steve, but then, within seconds of stepping out on to the pavement, there had been that visible spark of panic. What had caused it? Or, more to the point, who?

James activated his car's safety locks and got in, his dark eyes thoughtful as he contemplated the scene again. Something had

100

most definitely spooked her! He didn't switch on the ignition and drive off as he'd first intended. Instead, sitting back on the leather upholstery, he forced a picture of the street back into his memory, turning back to that particular moment in time. There had been the usual mixed bag of shoppers about that day, and Josie's panic-stricken eyes had been turned in the direction of the roundabout, towards the superstore. James focused hard. Had there been anything different about it, anything unusual?

It had all happened so quickly. One minute Josie was standing by his car, and the next minute she had gone, flying down the street and disappearing around the nearest corner as if her life had depended on it. James frowned. Perhaps it had! At the time, and taken by surprise, he had only thrown a quick glance in the direction of her frozen attention. His main thoughts then had been to wonder what was wrong, why she had run off like that without even a word of goodbye.

James turned his scrutiny in that same direction now, down towards the roundabout and across to the supermarket. But now, like then, all he could see was a general mixture of ordinary people, women mostly, criss-crossing the parking area with their plastic bags and shopping trolleys.

He let out an impatient sigh. There had been absolutely nothing unusual about the scene. But then, without really knowing why, his mouth tightened. Was it his imagination, or was there something he couldn't quite define? A shape was beginning to form in his mind, a blurry shape, and then a face, too, a face he couldn't really see but, nevertheless, a face that was, somehow, vaguely familiar. James concentrated hard, but the features would not materialise in his mind's eye.

He changed tack, his memory now turning to Josie's conversation in the car. Would it give him a clue? She had seemed upset. Vaguely, he recalled that she had been telling him, in particular, about one of her landscapes. Hadn't she said something about it being one of the best she'd ever done? And hadn't she said how proud she had been of the fact that it had been awarded second place in an art competition? And hadn't she said something about the fact that it was now useless?

His eyes narrowed as he forced himself to remember. Why was it useless? James frowned, cursing himself for the fact that he had been only half-listening to her, his attention focusing more on the traffic which, on that particular day, had been unusually heavy. He could only recall snatches of what Josie had been saying.

'I ask you James,' she had choked angrily, 'who could do such a thing?'

'What have they done? What do you mean?' he remembered asking without much interest.

'Done? They've destroyed it, that's what they've done! Torn it to shreds!'

She had broken off at that point, and had spent the next few minutes gazing out of the car window and groping in her bag for a tissue to wipe away hot, angry tears. James remembered telling her to calm down, but she had ignored his advice, and moments later, had continued with her tirade.

'I'm convinced it's all to do with Megan Butler. I saw this boy, you see. He was running away from something, I'm sure of that. I thought at the time he was acting strangely, but I never thought . . .'

James cursed himself again. Why hadn't he paid more attention? All he could recall, as he'd stopped at the lights, was asking her, 'Where was this?'

'By the river! Oh, James, it must have been connected with Megan! It must, because it was on the very day she disappeared! Of course!'

Then Josie had gone quiet and it was quite a few moments later before he had heard her voice again. She had clutched his arm and urged him, 'Drop me off by Newby Street, James. I must tell Steve, show him what's left of my picture. He'll know what to do.'

James had turned into the main street and had pulled up at the end of Steve Butler's street as requested, and Josie, who had lapsed into another thoughtful silence, climbed out and had, at once, reacted in that strange, uncharacteristic way. The blurry shape hovered back into James's mind. He still could not distinguish who it was, but there was one thing he knew instinctively—the figure was male. If only it would become more clear, he was convinced that it was the shape of a man well known in Tyr Gwyn.

However, at that moment, the sound of his mobile phone interrupted his thoughts and, expecting it to be either the airline or Carrie, he answered straightaway. It was neither, and after a brief conversation with the caller, James's manner changed and he became suddenly sharp and businesslike. The discussion lasted for only a couple of minutes, with James's brisk questions receiving equally concise answers. When it had finished, he disconnected the line and immediately keyed in the Owens' number, relieved to find that Carrie was still there.

He asked to speak to her and, again, the conversation was brief, with James arranging to meet her later at Dell Cottage. When that was done, he tossed his phone into the glove compartment and switched on the engine, nosing his way out of the carpark and on to the Cardiff ring-road. The fine-drawn angles of his handsome face were now set into an intense, determined mask, and there was a tautness that seemed to gleam on his knuckles as he clenched the steering-wheel. Earlier, he had listened to his caller with keen attention and had no difficulty now in identifying the blurred figure that day at the crossroads.

He knew now exactly who it had been!

James pressed hard on the accelerator. He had things to do, things that could wait no longer. Once out of the city, he headed westwards towards the Cefn-Mawr Valley.

*   *   *

It was a little after six-thirty when Carrie arrived back at her cottage. The day with Jean had passed pleasantly enough, and when Natalie had gone, she had helped with the chores and, later, when school was over, she had played with the children while Jean had prepared their supper.

She went upstairs and took a quick shower, changing into fresh clothes so as to look her best for James. A brief glance at her watch told her he would be here any time, causing her to feel again that sudden, excited stirring of her heart. With a smile, Carrie closed her bedroom door and moved to the top of the stairs, noticing as she did so that Aunt Lorna's door had been left ajar. She went to close it but, pausing instinctively, opened it wider instead.

She moved into her aunt's room, her eyes falling immediately on the cabinet in the corner. Why was she being drawn to those wretched crystals? What was it about them that fascinated her so? Pulling open the door, she reached inside and drew out the cloth, spilling the shiny pieces of glass on to the old-fashioned counterpane on Lorna's bed.

As before, Carrie stared down at them. The light from the window was too faint to make them sparkle this time, and they looked nothing more than what they were, a small heap of glass fragments. She shook her head, still not comprehending why her aunt had set such store by them and, with another little smile, she picked them up and, once more, began to wrap them away in the cloth.

Then, totally unexpectedly, something happened! Again, as on that other occasion, that same watery scene began to manifest itself in her mind's eye, whirling before her as clear as day. Once more she could see the river, and the rushing water, and the two anguished figures—one, small, unclear, struggling at its edge, and the other, a taller figure, his mouth contorted as though screaming and yelling, but without sound, and then turning and running away. Then the scene receded, grew more confused and dim until there was nothing left of it any more, nothing but the small heap of glass splinters.

Carrie pressed the back of one shaking hand to her mouth, scooping up the crystals with the other. Vaguely, she heard a car drive up. It must be James. She bit her lip in an agony of indecision and frustration. Supposing it wasn't!

What if it was someone else—the taller figure at the river's edge? The person whom she now knew must have abducted Megan! What if that same figure now believed that she, Carrie, could see the whole thing in the crystal, just like her aunt had before her?

With a small cry she thrust the shards of glass back into the cupboard. What was the matter with her? She was allowing her imagination to go crazy! Chiding herself for her silliness, she thrust away her fears and tried desperately to discipline her thoughts as she turned to leave the room. Her visitor just had to be James! And in something less than twelve seconds she was answering the summons of the doorbell, throwing the door wide open and falling into his arms.

James was more than a little startled by his reception. He stroked her hair and held her close, listening to her gasping breath.

'Whatever is it, darling?' he asked, looking down into her bewildered eyes. 'What's happened?'

Carrie felt numb with weariness, and her eyes held his pleadingly, betraying the agony of her mind.

'James,' she began, 'the crystals!'

'Crystals?'

She nodded, and began to tell him in a rushed, garbled way what she had seen moments before, as ridiculous as it seemed. His reaction, when it came, was as she expected. She heard his long-drawn whistle of disbelief, then he swore softly.

'Shall we go inside?' he suggested, taking her hand gently into his own. 'Forgive me, I didn't mean it to appear as though I don't believe you. But I think we'd be better inside, don't you?'

'Yes, yes, of course.'

And with James's steadying arm around her, Carrie allowed herself to be led into the sitting-room. In spite of all her fears and forebodings, she was suddenly realising that he had called her darling!

'What do you suppose it all means, James?'

Carrie turned two anxious eyes towards him as they stood together.

'What? The crystals?'

'Yes. There must be something in it or why do I keep seeing the same scene? And the awful sense of . . . of . . .'

She broke off, hardly able to explain her emotions.

'I don't know,' he answered quietly. 'But it is very strange, I grant you. And more so when I tell you what I have discovered.'

Carrie glanced at him nervously.

'What have you discovered, James?'

Instead of answering her question directly, James slipped a hand over hers and held her close. He held her for a brief moment before placing his forefinger under her chin to lift her face to his. Then he spoke softly.

'I'd like you to come with me to Cefn-Mawr.'

She looked at him a little stupidly.

'I'll explain on the way. Will you come?'

'Yes, of course, I will, but why Cefn-Mawr?'

'Because that's where I think we will find the key to all the skeletons in this village's cupboard.'

CHAPTER NINE

James sped along the unlit country road towards Cefn-Mawr, and Carrie couldn't fail to notice his alarming speed.

'Do we have to go so fast?' she asked, glancing nervously out of the window.

'Sorry,' James apologised. 'I didn't realise.'

He smiled, patted her hand and slackened his speed.

'Is that better?'

Carrie nodded, returning his smile.

'Much better, thanks.'

The touch of his hand had felt warm, sending a new shock through her as if he were giving out tangible waves of excitement.

'You're not flying a plane now, you know,' she went on, still smiling, but adopting a tone which she hoped sounded like disapproval. 'These country lanes can be deceptive. You never know what's coming towards you round the next corner.'

'You're quite right,' he said. 'I'll drive no faster than this, I promise.'

More at ease, and for the next mile or so, Carrie found herself thinking of everything that had happened over the past few days.

Presently, she said, 'You said you'd explain why we are going to Cefn-Mawr. What is it all about, James?'

'It's about a phone call I received when I arrived back at Cardiff airport. That, and a few conclusions I've come to myself.'

'A phone call? Conclusions?'

'Yes.'

He began to sound more cautious as he went on to explain.

'It's a phone call I half-expected long before now and, when it came, it more or less confirmed that the conclusions I have been formulating, putting two and two together, proved that my instincts have been right all along.'

'You're talking in riddles, James. Who was the phone call from? And what have you been putting together?'

'The call was from Josie.'

'Josie?'

Carrie turned to him, her eyes widening in startled surprise.

'Good heavens! Where is she? How is she? What did she say?'

'She's OK, she's fine,' James reassured her, 'She's been keeping her head down. She's had to lie low for a while, but it all boils down to a painting she did some years ago, and the fact that the painting, quite unintentionally, held the vital key to what happened to Megan Butler. That's all I can tell you at the moment. I don't know all the facts myself yet.'

Carrie felt a twisting in her heart.

'There must be more! What has Josie's

painting to do with Megan? And why has she had to lie low? James, tell me, is she in danger?'

'Calm down, love. I promise you, she's not in any immediate danger, at least, not for now. I've told you, she's fine,' he repeated. 'I'm just glad she's rung me at last, and, soon, you'll hear for yourself what she has to say.'

'Is Josie at Cefn-Mawr? Is that why we're going there?'

James gave a brief nod.

'Yes, and look, here we are.'

The car turned off the road, threading its way through the wrought-iron gates of a small lodge. Carrie could hear the whisper of moss as the tyres slowed down on the drive.

She knew the place. It had belonged to a late, distant relative of Josie's and had been up for sale for months. As they neared the sturdy, stone-built house, she saw a lace curtain at one of the ground-floor windows twitch and fall straight again. They got out of the car and, almost immediately, the front door opened to expose a dim light from the hallway, the light casting a shadow across the porch and silhouetting a slim figure who was standing there, awaiting their arrival. The figure ran forward, greeting her visitors with a strangled little cry.

'James! Carrie! Am I glad to see you!'

Josie Barnes hugged them both before leading them indoors. Once inside, James and

Carrie followed her down an unlit, narrow passage until they reached a sitting-room at the rear of the house, and as they entered it she moved over to a small, round table and lifted the cosy off a teapot.

'As you can see, I've been expecting you,' she told them with a smile as she set out the cups. 'Never let it be said that I would neglect a guest, no matter what the circumstances are. And, anyway, I felt sure you would welcome one once you got here. I'm sorry if you prefer coffee, but I'm all out of it. This place is at the back of beyond and the shops are miles away.'

She handed Carrie a cup.

'Will it do?'

'Of course it'll do, Josie. And it's very welcome indeed. Thanks.'

Carrie took the cup, eyeing up her long-time friend. She was feeling so relieved to see her again, relieved and yet still puzzled. The three of them settled down, sipping their tea and chatting over more mundane matters for the next few minutes until, unable to wait any longer, Carrie pressed on with her questions.

'Josie,' she urged, 'what's been happening? Why did you disappear the way you did? And why haven't you been in touch with any of us? We've all been so worried.'

The young woman gave another small smile, this time one of apology.

'I'm sorry, Carrie,' Josie murmured. 'Hasn't James explained?'

Carrie glanced up at him as he sat perched on the corner of the table.

'Well, hardly. He hasn't told me anything that makes any sense. I've really no idea what's going on. Will one of you please tell me what a painting of yours, Josie, has to do with Megan?'

James placed his cup down on the table and moved to sit on the arm of Carrie's chair, slipping an arm lightly around her shoulders.

'That's your cue, Jo,' he said quietly. 'We would both like to hear what you have to say. I understand now about the painting, but, like Carrie here, there's also a lot I don't know.'

'Yes, that painting. That was the start of the whole, terrible business.'

Josie Barnes sighed and set her cup and saucer on a table by her side.

'I must say, it will be a relief to get it all off my chest.'

She paused for a moment, then, slowly, she began.

'On the day little Megan drowned, I had gone up to Ty Mynydd to finish off some sketches for an art competition I had entered. I needed to fill in a few details before I committed the whole lot to a finished water-colour. Anyway, I had found my spot and had started to work. I must have been working away for about an hour. I remember thinking I had better hurry as the light was going. From my vantage point up on the mountainside and through the trees, I could see the river below.'

She paused, her face turning quite pale, and Carrie prompted her gently.

'Did you see something, Josie?'

Josie nodded.

'Yes, I did, but it's all so long ago. I was only twelve years old myself at the time, remember.'

She took a deep breath as if to steady herself.

'My heart and soul was entirely wrapped up in that competition. It was so important to me, and I remember I was so engrossed in my work that it didn't register with me what I was seeing at the river's edge, but afterwards, when we all heard about Megan . . .'

'What did you see, Josie?' Carrie prompted again.

'Just take your time,' James advised. 'It's OK. There's no rush.'

Josie smiled tremulously and then went on.

'I saw two people, children. They were playing, or so I thought, and I remember thinking they would get into trouble if their parents knew they were there, so near the river. I couldn't see who they were, they were too far away, and one of them was in the water, swimming, as I thought. The other one, the older one, seemed to be jumping up and down and waving his arms about. I know I remember thinking that they must be playing some sort of stupid game, and that they must have been mad to be swimming that day. It was quite cold.'

Carrie shivered. She, too, had turned cold. Josie was describing exactly what she had seen in the crystals! James must have felt her shiver because his arm tightened around her and she heard him say, 'Go on, Josie, you're doing fine.'

'Well, that's all, really. As I said, the light was going fast and I packed up my gear soon afterwards. I remember looking back towards the river but the two figures had gone, and I thought that was the end of it, until later that day, when we heard about Megan, I realised it must have been her in the water. I've had nightmares about it since. At the time I did mention what I had seen to the policemen who were doing the investigation and they asked me to describe the other person on the bank, but I couldn't.'

She threw them a brief, desperate, glance.

'I had no idea who it was. They were both too far away. In fact, I couldn't even be sure that it was Megan. For all I knew it could have been any two kids from anywhere, and nothing to do with Megan at all.'

Josie paused again, glancing first at Carrie and then at James. She seemed to be relieved that it was out in the open at last, and yet her tension had been such that the relief was making little impression on her. She sat there, her hands balled into two tight little fists, and a deep frown line had etched itself between her worried eyes.

'It was years later,' she went on quietly after a moment, 'very recently, in fact, that it all came back to haunt me. I had some friends round to my house, Natalie, Mark, Steve and some of the girls. We were planning the next show, and having a glass or two of wine. Anyway, as always happens, when we finished talking about who would be playing what, the conversation moved on to other things, and someone, I can't remember who, asked me if I was still painting. I remember telling whoever it was that I hadn't painted anything decent for ages. Then Steve, always the flatterer, said that wasn't true and that I ought to take it up seriously again. He said that I had too much talent to throw away and, to prove it, he asked me to show the others some of my early work. As you know, Steve is—'

She corrected herself.

'Was quite an artist himself. Anyway, I was flattered enough to go upstairs and dig out my folios. I took down the whole lot, about twelve in all, some completed and some still just sketches. Looking back, it was the worst thing I could have done.'

'Why?' Carrie asked very quietly.

Josie stared at Carrie, her mouth twisting in a wry smile.

'Because one of them was the drawing I had started at the river that day. I hadn't realised that I'd actually sketched in the two children, but they were there as clear as day, one in the water and one at the water's edge, just as I'd seen them. So you see, subconsciously, I'd drawn them in as part of the scene, and there was no mistaking who they were.'

Carrie shivered.

'Ah, I think I see now.'

Josie continued.

'And among that group of friends in my house, looking at the picture with the others, was the boy, now grown up, who had been watching Megan that day, in the river.'

Her voice began to shake.

'And, of course, that same grown-up little boy recognised the scene. And, from then on, he's made my life a misery. He sees me as a danger, which I am, of course, because I now know the truth. Twice now he's tried to cause me to have an accident.'

Carrie felt suddenly sick. She clutched her shaking hands together and tried desperately to retain her sense of reason.

'What did he do, Josie? How did he try to hurt you?'

Josie, stumbling over her words, began to tell them of the time she was convinced that someone had tried to run her down on the road outside her home, and how she'd had to fling herself backwards from the path of the faceless driver; and of the other time when her brake fluid had run dry on the evening she'd taken the mountain road into Cardiff, and she'd had to veer off on to the verge, and only just made it by the skin of her teeth. She'd used her mobile phone for a garage to come out and collect her. Her own garage had only serviced her car that very morning.

'Did this person know you were going that way, taking the mountain road?' James asked grimly.

'Oh, yes,' Josie replied immediately. 'I'd told everyone at the rehearsal that afternoon. They'd all joked about my car being too old for it.'

It seemed an age before anyone spoke, and then Josie, hesitantly, took up the tale again.

'And I believe that because this man knew that Steve had recognised him on that drawing, too, that he had to do something about him also. He must have been the one who tampered with Steve's brakes.'

Josie's fragile composure was now completely gone, and Carrie, trembling, leaned across and put her hand over her friend's in a gesture of comfort and support. After a few moments Josie looked up, her eyes filled with tears.

'My life is still in danger and I can't stand it anymore.'

There was another short, electric silence. Carrie was stunned, shocked and speechless, unable to meet either Josie's or James's eyes. She sat very still, her face registering the horror of the scene, the same scene that had haunted her for these last weeks. Then the colour began to flood back into her face and she felt her cheeks burn scarlet. Everything she had seen in her aunt's fragments of glass had just been confirmed by Josie, and the taller figure at the river that day had been the cause of Megan Butler's drowning.

From somewhere far away, she heard the reassuring voice of James as he asked, 'It'll soon be over, Josie, I promise you. But just one more thing. Can you tell us now the name of the boy who was at the river that day?'

Carrie saw Josie shudder.

'The boy? Yes, yes, of course I can.'

'Who was it?'

Two pairs of eyes were watching her as she struggled to pull herself together, and when she finally answered it was in a tone that was almost normal.

'It was Mark—Mark Jones. Not long after our little get-together at my house, when they'd all seen the drawings, he came back to see me and asked to see the drawing again. Like a fool and not thinking properly, I went and got it from upstairs again. He was furious when he looked at it! He said it had been an accident, and that he hadn't meant to leave Megan in the water for her to drown. He panicked, and he said that it had been hard enough to live with all these years without me bringing it all out in the open again in an old, forgotten picture.'

'Did he say how Megan had got up there with him in the first place?' James interrupted.

'Yes, he did. He said he had gone to call for Steve but he hadn't been at home. He said he'd seen Megan playing with her doll in the garden and that when he left she must have followed him. Apparently, she always loved to be with her brother and his friends. Anyway, Mark said he didn't realise she was there until much later, when he was almost at the river. And when he did finally see her, she told him she'd been playing a game of hide-and-seek, as she always did with Steve.'

'What a terrible, terrible tragedy.'

Carrie felt her heart bumping rapidly as she pushed her hair back from her forehead. In her mind's eye she could see again two children playing on a river's bank, one never to return, and the other to bear the burden of guilt and failure for ever.

'Was it Mark who destroyed the painting?' James asked.

'Yes, it must have been. I can't think of anyone else who had a reason to. He obviously got into my house whilst I was out and tried to get rid of the evidence, which he did, of course, because I could never put it in for exhibition again.'

She gave a deep, despairing sigh.

'Worst of all though, I'd already told Steve about it and Mark knew that, so that put him in danger, too.'

'Is that why you ran away?' Carrie asked.

Josie nodded.

'Yes. I didn't know what else to do. I thought if I stayed away Mark would think the danger to himself would be over. I was wrong, of course. I should have spoken out from the beginning.'

She glanced at James.

'That's when I finally rang you, James.'

He grinned a little wryly.

'You took your time about it.'

'I know. It was when I came across a copy of the local paper and read of Steve's accident that I realised I had already waited far too long.'

'You did what you thought was right at the time,' James said quietly.

Carrie looked up at his profile, just inches away from her own. There was compassion in his eyes but also something else, a hint of wariness, of reserve, of speculation.

'What is to be done now, James?' she asked him.

'We must tell the police everything,' he answered. 'What happened to Megan was probably, as Mark himself admits, a terrible accident that caused him to panic. We must remember he was hardly more than a child himself. However, we mustn't lose track of the fact that he has since harassed and threatened you, Josie. And although we can't prove it yet, it looks very much as though he caused Steve's accident, too. And that was definitely not the act of a frightened child.'

He shook his head.

'No, as long as Mark Jones thinks he can get away, quite literally, with murder, then you will never be safe.'

He glanced soberly across at Josie.

'There's no question about it. We must tell the police all we know. Do you feel up to it?'

'Yes, James,' Josie replied. 'I'm up to it.'

CHAPTER TEN

After months of postponement, it seemed the entire population of Tyr Gwyn had turned out to see Natalie's production of West Side Story finally reach the stage, and now that the show had reached its finale the applause was exuberant and wholehearted. With the unanimous approval of the village, the show had been dedicated to the memory of the unfortunate little Megan, and its proceeds were to go to the development of a small playing area to be named after her.

There was now no doubt the cast's efforts had turned out to be a tremendous success! Carrie beamed delightedly towards the show's gratified producer and watched Natalie take her bows.

Almost a year had passed by since Mark Jones had confessed to his part in the drowning of little Megan Butler, and, later, to the stalking of Josie and to tampering with Steve Butler's car. When questioned by the police he didn't even try to deny it, and especially after learning that his fingerprints had been found on a metal rod inside Steve's car's engine. Within two days of the police enquiry, he had walked into the police station voluntarily and the matter had been drawn to its conclusion.

Months later, when the case was heard, the jury had been sympathetic to the first count, bringing in a verdict of accidental death. But to the second and third counts concerning Steve and Josie, Mark was sentenced accordingly but with the added recommendation that he receive counselling and suitable treatment.

The applause was still thundering in Carrie's ears as she felt James's arm slip around her shoulder, bringing her thoughts back to the present.

'Well, love,' he murmured in her ear, 'that turned out OK, didn't it? Shall we join the others at the White Hart to celebrate the show's success?'

And so it was, a little less than an hour later, that James and Carrie were seated together at their favourite table in Tyr Gwyn's popular little pub. Jean and Dave, Natalie, Ian, Adele Parry and everyone who had had a hand in the show's success were there to celebrate. Josie was there, too, looking better than she had done in a long time. Her nightmare adventure was resolved now, and time had begun its healing process. True, she would never be quite the same again. She would miss Steve, but that deep, dull aching she had felt over the last few months would also fade with time.

'It looks as though Ian and Adele are getting along quite well,' Carrie heard James say as he glanced over to a nearby table to where the two of them were sitting. 'They made a rather good Tony and Maria after all.'

Carrie's eyes drifted towards them. They did indeed seem to be getting on very well together. They were laughing softly, heads close together, as though sharing some special secret, and the expressions on their faces were not hiding the fact that they were enjoying each other's company very much.

'Yes,' Carrie agreed, 'they were extremely good. But then, she's a very lovely girl, isn't she? Perfect for the part.'

'Mm, very lovely.'

Carrie turned to look at James.

'I thought you rather liked her yourself once.'

'I did. She's very attractive, but it was only a passing phase. Trouble was, I'd already seen someone else who attracted me more.'

'Oh?' Carrie asked, curious. 'And who was that?'

'As if you didn't know. Anyway, shall we make our excuses to go now?'

Carrie glanced at her watch.

'So soon?'

'I doubt they'll miss us.'

'Well, if you say so.'

Carrie glanced around at the noisy, laughing crowd.

'At least when they see us leave this early it will give them something else to talk about,' she commented.

They rose and said their good-nights, and as they pressed their way towards the door Carrie couldn't help but notice Jean's knowing wink.

'You two off then?' she asked.

'Yes. I'll ring you tomorrow, Jean.'

'Make sure you do, but not too early, please. The kids are at my mother's so Dave and I are hoping for a lie-in.'

'You're not leaving already?' Natalie chimed in, her eyes bright with excitement and champagne.

'Yes, I hope you don't mind.'

Natalie leaned over to brush a light kiss across Carrie's cheek.

'Not at all. It means more champagne for me. I've earned it, I think.'

'No-one more so, Natalie. Well, good-night then.'

James's arm pressed more tightly around Carrie's waist as he propelled her forward.

'Well done, Nat! Roll on the next show,' he said sincerely.

'And I take it I can rely on the two of you to help again with our next production?'

'You have our word.'

At Dell Cottage, James and Carrie stood close together by the curtained window of the sitting-room. His arms were around her, and his cheek rested against her hair.

'I've been thinking,' he began.

'Oh, dear,' Carrie murmured. 'That could be a dangerous occupation.'

127

He grinned.

'No, seriously, I've been thinking that although we've known each other for just a few short months, we've shared quite a number of incidents.'

'That's true,' she agreed, 'and quite scary ones, too, for the most part.'

'You're not scared of me, I hope.'

Carrie laughed.

'Of course not.'

She felt the warmth of his lips as they brushed against her hair.

'In fact, James, I'm glad you were here. With everything that's happened I don't know how I would have coped without you.'

He lifted her face to his and kissed her lightly on the lips.

'You would have coped very well. Your aunt always knew that.'

'Do you really think so?"

'I do.'

Her gaze followed his to Aunt Lorna's photograph, and for several moments they stood silently together, each one thinking of the old lady who, in her mysterious way, had brought them together.

'I hope the things I saw in her crystal were really mere coincidence. I never wanted her special gift. I don't think I could live with it,' Carrie said.

'You won't have to, darling,' James told her soberly. 'I want you to live with me. Do you think you could?'

Carrie's eyes held his, a hint of mischief showing itself in her joy.

'Is that a proposal?'

'Yes,' he said simply, and kissed her again.

'Then I accept,' Carrie responded.

'Well, then, that's settled.'

'Not quite.'

'Why not?' He grinned. 'It was a very nice proposal, wasn't it?'

'Yes, very nice, but there are a couple of things I'm still not sure about.'

'Such as?' James asked, puzzled.

'Well, where will we live, for one thing?'

'Here, of course, at Dell Cottage,' he replied.

'But what about your place, after all the work you've put into it?'

'We'll sell it,' he said at once. 'This is the place for us. Lorna always intended it to be, Now, what's the other thing?'

'Other thing?'

'You said there were a couple of things you weren't sure about.'

This time, Carrie didn't answer him right away. Instead, she moved away and went to stand by the fireplace, looking down into the unlit logs and betraying a little discomfort. She stood gazing down for several moments.

'What shall we do with the crystals?' she asked eventually.

James moved across to stand by her side.

129

'What do you want to do with them?'

'I honestly don't know.'

'Then we'll do nothing. After all, they're as much a part of the cottage, and us, as anything else. Don't be afraid, darling. We'll just keep them where they are until, one day, we'll know what to do.'

She glanced at him with a smile.

'I suppose that's all we can do.'

'Yes, for now, it is.'

He turned her towards him and held her close, the look of love on his face almost causing her to cry out.

'By the way,' he went on, 'did I ever tell you just how much I love you?'

Carrie laughed, her heart singing.

'No, you didn't, not until now, and I love you, too, James, very much.'

'Surely, you must have known I loved you.'

Carrie laughed again, devilment in her eyes.

'Perhaps I saw it in the crystals,' she said wistfully as he drew her once more into his arms.